T0125514

THE ROAD TO MADISON

What Reviewers Say About Elle Spencer's Work

Unforgettable

"Across both novellas, Elle Spencer delivers four distinct, compelling leads, as well as interesting supporting casts that round out their stories. If you like angsty romances, this is the book for you! Both stories pack a punch, with so much "will they or won't they" that I kind of wondered how they'd turn out (yes, even though it's marketed as romance!)"—*The Lesbian Review*

"I was stunned at how Elle Spencer manages to make the reader feel so much and we end up really caring for the women in her novels. …This book is perfect for those times you want to wallow in romance, intense feelings and love. Elle Spencer does it so well."—*Kitty Kat's Book Review Blog*

Casting Lacey

"The characters have a chance to really get to know each other, becoming friends and caring for each other before their feelings turn romantic. It also allows for a whole lot of angst that keeps things interesting. *Casting Lacey* is a compelling, sexy, angsty romance that I highly recommend to anyone who's into fake relationship books or celebrity romances. It kept me sucked in and I'm looking forward to seeing more from Elle Spencer in the future."—*The Lesbian Review*

"This is a very good debut novel that combines the fake girlfriend trope with celebrity lifestyle. …The characters are well portrayed and have off the charts chemistry. The story is full of humour, wit and saucy dialogues but also has angst and drama. I think that the book is at its best in the humorous parts which are really well written. …An entertaining and enjoyable read."—*Lez Review Books*

"This is the romance I've been recommending to everyone and her mother since I read it, because it's basically everything I've been dying to find in an f/f romance—funny voices I click with, off-the-charts chemistry, a later-in-life coming out, and a host of fun tropes from fake dating to costars."—*Frolic*

Visit us at www.boldstrokesbooks.com

By the Author

Casting Lacey

Unforgettable

The Road to Madison

THE ROAD TO MADISON

by

Elle Spencer

2019

THE ROAD TO MADISON

© 2019 BY ELLE SPENCER. ALL RIGHTS RESERVED.

ISBN 13: 978-1-63555-421-2

THIS TRADE PAPERBACK ORIGINAL IS PUBLISHED BY
BOLD STROKES BOOKS, INC.
P.O. BOX 249
VALLEY FALLS, NY 12185

FIRST EDITION: MAY 2019

THIS IS A WORK OF FICTION. NAMES, CHARACTERS, PLACES, AND INCIDENTS ARE THE PRODUCT OF THE AUTHOR'S IMAGINATION OR ARE USED FICTITIOUSLY. ANY RESEMBLANCE TO ACTUAL PERSONS, LIVING OR DEAD, BUSINESS ESTABLISHMENTS, EVENTS, OR LOCALES IS ENTIRELY COINCIDENTAL.

THIS BOOK, OR PARTS THEREOF, MAY NOT BE REPRODUCED IN ANY FORM WITHOUT PERMISSION.

CREDITS
EDITOR: BARBARA ANN WRIGHT
PRODUCTION DESIGN: SUSAN RAMUNDO
COVER DESIGN BY TAMMY SEIDICK

Acknowledgments

As always, many thanks to Rad, Sandy and the entire Bold Strokes team, for your incredible support and for making the publishing process so easy.

Thanks also to my editors, Barbara Ann Wright and Stacia Seaman, for your invaluable insight and guidance along the way.

To my fellow Bold Strokes authors who provide me with inspiration and motivation, I'm blessed to be in such great company.

Counselor, I can't thank you enough for all of your help with this book. It's better because of you. Also, thank you for being the best friend I could ever ask for. #rideordie

Nikki, it is only with your love, support, and patience that I'm able to bring this book to life. Thank you for being the first one to read the rough drafts. The first one to edit all the bad grammar. The first one to say, this is great, keep going. I know you're just as excited as I am to introduce Madison and Ana to the world, and that makes me love you even more than I already do. #bestwife

And to the readers, I am so grateful to you for continuing to read my words, and for all of the encouragement along the way. I wouldn't be here without you.

CHAPTER ONE

I need an hour."

"Ma'am..." The gravedigger paused when he saw the two crisp hundred-dollar bills in Madison's hand. "I'm really not allowed—"

"Please," she interrupted. "I'm just not ready to say good-bye yet. You understand, don't you?" She glanced at his name tag. "Willard?"

"Yes, ma'am." He took the tip and gestured for his helper to follow him. "We'll be back in an hour to finish up."

"Thank you, Willard." Madison scanned the area, making sure none of the attendees had lingered. They hadn't. No surprise there. She saw her own car parked in the nearby drive. Stephen, her driver, had the good sense to focus his attention elsewhere. He sat in the driver's seat, staring intently at his phone.

Apart from Madison and Stephen, the cemetery seemed to be empty, and why wouldn't it be, given the chill in the air? This was hardly a good day to visit deceased loved ones, but it was a perfect day to bury one.

She removed the black leather gloves from her slender fingers and tucked them into her coat pocket. She removed her coat next and folded it over the back of a chair. This would probably ruin her dress. Good. She'd burn it later in the fireplace.

She ran her fingers over the string of pearls around her neck. Should she remove them? They were a gift, after all, but no. If they got sullied, so be it. She'd burn them too. That left the dark sunglasses. She tossed them on the chair and turned toward the gravesite.

Madison Prescott was thirty-six years old and sole heir to her family's fortune. As of today, she had officially assumed control of the Prescott estate. On Monday, the board would vote to make her the next CEO of Prescott Industries. It was a formality, she knew. She'd been interim CEO for the past six months, and besides, everyone knew Madison Prescott had been groomed for the role her entire life. First though, she had other fish to fry.

She'd interrupted the gravedigger. The poor guy was only doing his job, but that hadn't stopped her. The moment her father's casket had been lowered into the ground, she'd opened her wallet.

Now as she stood above the gravesite, looking down at the dark oak casket that so closely resembled the humidor sitting on his desk, she found herself wondering if he'd purposely chosen to be laid to rest in a replica of the possession that was most important to him. She tucked her hair behind her ears and took a deep breath. She was ready. So very ready.

The first handful of dirt hit the casket like a gentle rainfall as she spread her fingers. It was an odd tradition, the throwing of dirt. Madison knew it was supposed to be some sort of symbolic closure for Catholics, like her father claimed to be. Still, she wondered if the person who thought up this little ritual wanted to do it for the same reasons she did. She picked up another handful, then another. On the third throw, everything changed. It felt as though the air had been sucked from her body. The perfume that lingered in the air was unmistakable.

"Ana," she whispered.

"Madison."

Madison's throat constricted. Eyes that had been dry since her father's death filled with tears. She turned around and tried to find her voice. "Thank you for coming."

Ana turned her attention to the hole in the ground. "I'm not here for you. I'm here for me. I had to see it for myself."

Madison could barely speak, but Ana's voice was forceful, her tone cold. The words cut to the core. She knew she had to accept them. How could she not, after all that had happened? Besides, there was no time to ask for forgiveness. Willard would be back soon.

Madison grabbed a shovel. With the pointed toe of her black, stiletto heel, she pushed deep into the dirt pile and threw the biggest shovelful she could manage. It hit George Prescott's casket with a loud thump. She paused for a moment. Her lip quivered so hard, she had to cover it with her hand.

This was supposed to be easy. Just bury the son of a bitch, wipe your hands clean, and move on with life. Madison wanted to see Ana again, but not like this. Not now. Not *here*. Madison choked back a sob and filled the shovel again, trying to ignore the scent of Ana's perfume lingering in the air.

Ana stepped up to the grave. She peered down at the casket and then met Madison's gaze. "May I join you?"

Madison gave a nod, not sure exactly what Ana had in mind. It didn't matter because at least Ana had looked her in the eye when she'd said the words. That was something, wasn't it?

Ana removed her coat. Apparently, she hadn't bothered to wear black. In fact, she looked as if she'd just come from work in a gray pencil skirt and white silk blouse. She grabbed another shovel, dug into the pile, and without hesitation, threw it on the casket.

Were they really going to do this together, or was it just a symbolic thing? Would one shovelful be enough? Madison watched in shock as Ana filled her shovel again. No, one shovelful was definitely not enough. Madison dug deep into the pile again, and without words, the two impeccably dressed women threw shovel after shovelful of dirt on top of George Madison Prescott III.

With most of the dirt pile gone, Madison threw the shovel to the side and wiped her sweaty brow. It was done. And if anyone ever reported what she'd just done, burying her father herself instead of letting someone else do it, she had an excuse ready. It was her job, as his only child, to give him the final respect he so deserved, she'd tell them. Sure, she doubted anyone would believe her excuse—that she just couldn't bear to let a stranger do it, but she also doubted anyone would care enough to question it.

After they finished the task, Ana turned and started to walk away. Madison caught her sleeve, leaving a dirty handprint on the silk. "Could you stay a minute longer?"

Ana seemed to stiffen at the touch. She put her coat over her arm and held her chin high. "No. I got what I came here for."

There was that cold tone again. Madison had never heard it before today. She wiped her cheek with the back of her dirty hand. She couldn't stop the flow of tears she'd managed to keep at bay since the doctor gave the final nod, indicating her father had taken his last breath. Now, the tears flowed freely. If she could just stop crying, maybe she could tell Ana how sorry she was. How her only respite in fifteen years had been the few minutes she allowed herself in the shower each morning to imagine that things had turned out differently. If only she could explain. But those words were stuck behind the gigantic lump in her throat.

She was trying to think of a way to keep Ana there a little longer when the unthinkable happened. Ana turned back to the grave, stepped forward, and spat on it. When she turned back around, their eyes met for a few seconds. Ana's were so full of anger and hate, Madison had to turn away. She waited until she heard a car door open and close before she turned back around. Ana was gone.

Spitting wasn't something Madison Prescott ever did. But it seemed so damned appropriate, didn't it? Yes. Ana had that much right. And if she could somehow honor Ana and disparage her father at the same time, well, that would be time well spent.

She put her sunglasses back on. She put her coat over her arm and stepped back over to the grave. How does one spit? *Just pretend you're brushing your teeth. Spit out the toothpaste.* Sweat dripped down her back. Her hairline was soaked, but her mouth was bone dry. Hell, it could wait. The old man wasn't going anywhere.

She turned to walk away, then thought better of it. Madison walked back to the gravesite and spat on her father's coffin as if God meant for her to do it. And she suspected He did.

Stephen opened the car door for his boss and then got in the driver's seat. He couldn't believe what he'd just witnessed—Madison Prescott burying her father with her bare hands? It was unbelievable. He had no idea what to say to her, how to comfort her.

Then there was the woman who had parked the sports car behind him. He hadn't seen her at the funeral, but from what he'd just witnessed, he had a pretty good idea who she was.

Ana Perez.

Stephen knew about Ana. Everyone knew about Ana. He'd heard the story many times, told by different members of the staff who had been there at the time. The details were usually different, depending on how salaciously a particular staff member wanted to tell it, but the ending was always the same—forbidden love gone horribly wrong.

He'd almost missed seeing her get out of her car, more concerned with texting for updates on his daughter's school play. When he'd heard the car door open and close behind him,

Stephen rolled down his window to get a better look. It wasn't like him to intrude in this way, but in the Prescott household, Madison and Ana had the mystique of Prince Edward and Wallis Simpson. The difference, of course, being that Madison hadn't abdicated the family throne for love.

Stephen had watched the woman walk toward the gravesite with her head held high. She looked as if she belonged at Mr. Prescott's funeral, with her expensive German car and her designer clothes. That surprised Stephen since the Ana Perez he'd heard about was a maid's daughter. With her short, sculpted hair and sunglasses so large they covered most of her face, she looked more like some of the executives Madison often lunched with.

One thing was clear, the woman knew how to bury a dead man.

Stephen waited patiently for instructions. He didn't want to start the car until Madison was ready to leave. They sat in silence for what felt like an eternity. He finally cleared his throat. "Madison?"

Stephen always said her name with hesitation in his voice. She insisted that he, and all the other staff, for that matter, call her by her first name, not Ms. Prescott. After all they'd been through, he ought to be fine with it, but Stephen was a socially awkward sort. He'd always been most comfortable with a very clear set of rules to follow, so he usually addressed her as "ma'am."

This time was different, though. He'd just witnessed about as traumatic a moment as he'd ever seen Madison involved in, and a furtive glance in the review mirror revealed a boss who was doing everything she could to keep from sobbing. He had a pretty good idea that those tears weren't for George M. Prescott *the damned third.* The pompous bastard lived for that damned suffix, making sure everyone knew he was "American royalty." So what if he could trace his heritage back to the Revolutionary

War? It was Stephen's opinion that the only person who cared was the man himself.

With no reply from the backseat, Stephen continued to wait, worried that maybe he hadn't said her name loud enough. He'd often been told that he spoke too softly. Never by Madison. She only ever had kind, encouraging words for him. But other people, mostly Mr. Prescott, would rudely tell him to "speak up, son!" He hated the way he would jump when Mr. Prescott spoke to him that way, but the truth was, the man scared him to death, and he was glad he was gone.

Stephen glanced in the rearview mirror again. Madison was staring out the window, covering her quivering mouth with the edge of her index finger. He could see a tear running down her cheek, and he wanted to get in the back seat and hold her in his arms. Tell her everything would be fine like she'd done for him so many times. But he was just her driver. Not family. Not even friends. Just a driver. He swallowed the lump in his throat and willed himself to hold back his own tears.

It had been a hard week for everyone. Though Stephen felt crass thinking about it in those terms, the week had been made that much harder by a future that was suddenly unclear. Would Madison keep the Prescott estate and all of the staff that was required to keep it running, or would she downsize and move to the city? Everyone on the estate was on edge about it, and they all wanted Stephen to address their concerns. But he couldn't. Madison hadn't said a word about it, and he wasn't going to ask. It wasn't his place to ask.

"How did she do?" Their eyes met in the rearview mirror. "Kelsey. The school play," Madison added. "I'm sorry you had to miss it."

Stephen cleared his throat, choking back his emotions. *Madison knew?* And with everything she'd been going through, she cared enough to ask? His boss never ceased to amaze him. "Sarah said she did good. And I wouldn't be anywhere else today." He took a deep breath and blinked several times, but he couldn't hold back the tears. He grabbed a handkerchief out of his pocket and dabbed his eyes. "I'm sorry, ma'am. Just give me a moment."

❖

Madison wasn't in a hurry to go anywhere. She'd planned this moment for fifteen years. It always ended with her in the same place: at the doorstep of the girl she had loved her entire life. Ana would open the door. And then, Ana would open her arms. How naïve did Madison have to be to think it would all go that smoothly?

That was the dream that had kept Madison going all these years. How could it have never occurred to her that Ana hated her with the same amount of passion she used to love her?

Of course, she knew exactly how she could have overlooked that minor detail. The Ana she'd known had never hated anyone. Today, for the first time, Madison saw that the girl she'd known was gone—replaced by a woman who had traded in trust for suspicion and love for disdain. This version of Ana was entirely Madison's creation. And God, how it hurt.

Madison opened the car door, got out, and ran. She ran at full speed between the gravestones, trying to escape the pain, but she didn't get very far. Her heel breaking off in the damp grass brought her to her knees. She looked up at the sky and screamed, "Goddamn you!" Gasping for breath between sobs, she screamed it again. "Goddamn you, George!"

Stephen walked up to her and knelt down on one knee. "Ma'am," he whispered, his own voice filled with emotion. "I'm…I'm here."

Madison took his offered hand and squeezed it as she heaved for air. He helped her to her feet. She took off one shoe and then the other. Stephen took them from her hand. "Let me."

Madison leaned heavily on Stephen as they walked back to the car in silence. She steadied herself on the car door and turned to take one more look at her father's grave. She could hear him in her head, expressing his disgust with her for showing any emotion. *Get a hold of yourself,* he would say. *You're a goddamned Prescott. Start acting like it.*

"You don't get to tell me who to be anymore, Dad," she said under her breath.

"Ma'am?"

Madison shook her head. "Nothing, Stephen. Let's go home."

CHAPTER TWO

A na knew it was wrong to spit on someone's grave. Even if that someone was George Prescott. Her mother would be disappointed in her. That was a given. She'd probably insist Ana go to confession, even though the only times she stepped into a church were on Christmas and Easter. Even then, it was only so her mother wouldn't have to go alone. Maybe she'd just leave out the spitting part when she told her mother that he was really dead. That bastard, George Prescott, was really dead.

She imagined the confession she'd never go to. *Forgive me, Father, for I have sinned. It's been...um...seventeen years since my last confession. The love of my life's father died. I spit on his grave and didn't have a single word of comfort for his daughter. But really, Father, I have a good excuse!* Ana looked down at her ruined manicure and shook her head. "There's never a good excuse, my child," she said in a low voice, imitating a priest from her childhood.

"Hi there, Ms. Perez," Ana's doorman, Tommy, called out in his typically chipper tone. "How's it go—" He trailed off as Ana came closer. He looked her up and down. "You all right, miss?"

Ana glanced down at herself. Oh God. She was a disaster. Her Manolo Blahniks were ruined. She stamped her feet a few times to get the clods of dirt off before walking through the door

Tommy held open. *Note to self: Next time you bury a body, don't wear eight-hundred-dollar heels.* "I'm fine, Tommy. You should see the other guy." Tommy gave her a confused smile and let the matter go.

In the elevator, she looked at the blister that was forming on the palm of her hand. She'd felt it at the time but couldn't seem to stop shoveling dirt on that awful man. She could live with a blister. It was temporary. The satisfaction she felt would be permanent. She made the sign of the cross as the elevator door opened, hoping God would grant her a little mercy today.

Inside her east side apartment, Ana kicked her heels off by the front door so she wouldn't track dirt onto the glossy white tile. She couldn't get undressed fast enough, leaving a trail of clothing behind her as she made her way to the shower. She didn't particularly care about showering off the dirt. It was *her*— freaking Madison Prescott and the feelings she stirred up that needed to be washed away. And the sooner, the better.

She passed through her bedroom in nothing but her panties and stopped short when she saw movement in the bed. "Kris? What are you doing here?"

Ana's sometimes-on, sometimes-off girlfriend sat up. "How did it go?" She ran her fingers through her dark brown hair and blinked the sleep from her eyes.

"You don't need to be here," Ana said. "I'm fine."

Kris got out of bed and followed Ana into the bathroom. She sat on the vanity, tucking her hands under her bare legs. "Really? You're absolutely fine?"

"Don't make me take your key away."

"Like I haven't heard that threat before," Kris said.

"We're not dating anymore. You don't need to do this."

"Yeah, you've said that a few times too, but here I am, with a key to your place on my keyring. What was it you said? So I could let myself in when it's 'convenient'?" She made air quotes. "I guess what you meant was 'convenient for you.'"

Ana slipped her panties off and turned on the water, waiting for it to get hot before she stepped into the shower. She'd dated Kris on and off for three years, so of course, Kris knew the Madison Prescott story. And maybe being *fine* after what she'd just done wasn't in the cards, but why did Kris have to show up and throw it in her face?

That wasn't it. Ana knew that. Kris wasn't there to make her feel worse, but the last thing Ana wanted to do was talk about it. She turned to Kris and softened her tone. "You look beat. Long shift, doctor?"

Kris chuckled and looked at her watch. "It's Friday, right?"

"Go home. I'm fine." Ana stepped into the shower.

"You're not fine!" Kris shouted. "God, Ana."

Kris was right. Ana wasn't fine. She stifled a sob, hoping Kris wouldn't hear her over the water. The second sob she couldn't hold in. She gripped the sides of the shower and just as she lost the will to stand, Kris caught her and helped her to the floor.

❖

"I know what you're doing." Ana pushed her cup of tea away and leaned on the table.

"Oh, yeah?" Kris tucked her wet hair behind her ears. "What am I doing, Ana?"

"You're waiting for me to talk about it." She closed her eyes and lightly pressed on them. They were swollen from all of the crying. She couldn't go back to work looking like this. She couldn't sit here in silence for much longer, either.

Kris glanced at the trail of clothes leading to the bedroom. "A man you hated with a passion is dead, and you came home from the funeral looking like you buried him yourself—"

"We did," Ana said, interrupting her.

Kris blinked. "Did what?"

Ana pushed back from the table. She took her cup to the sink and poured it out, then turned and leaned against it. She tightened her bathrobe and folded her arms. "We buried George ourselves."

Kris shook her head in confusion. "Who did?"

"Me and Madison."

1992

Madison kicked a rock down the long drive to the main road. She knew there was no escaping. The huge iron gate would be locked, and she wasn't strong enough to open it on her own. Heaven knows she'd tried. She'd even tried squishing herself between the bars, but her head was too big.

Climbing over it wasn't an option, either. It was too slippery and too high. She'd learned that lesson the hard way a few days ago and had a bruised butt to prove it. If only there was someone she could show that bruise to now. Someone who would appreciate how gross it looked—all yellowish green and purple.

Her old nanny would tell her it was her own fault for being so silly. Her dad would just roll his eyes and go back to his newspaper. No, she needed someone who could truly appreciate the gore factor, but it was summer, and besides, she'd get into so much trouble for dropping her pants at school, even if it was just to show off the most awesomest bruise ever.

She stopped kicking her rock when she saw a little girl with dark brown braids running toward her. She squinted her eyes to get a better look. Her eyesight wasn't so good, but she hated wearing those dumb glasses all the time. And maybe they were broken, anyway, due to a fall from her favorite tree yesterday. So what, she thought. Life went on, even if she couldn't make out the leaves on the trees, and it was just one big, green blob. It was still a tree.

As the girl got closer, Madison had it figured out. She was the new maid's daughter. No one else would wear their jeans that short. High waters. That's what the kids at school called them. Chastising herself, she repeated what her mom had told her before she'd died. *Don't judge people by how much money they do or don't have, Maddy. Some of the worst people in the world have pockets full of cash, and some of the best people in the world don't have an extra penny to their name. Remember that.*

And Madison had. She'd already decided the new maid, Carmen, was a good person. Maybe her daughter wasn't half bad, either.

"Hi! I'm Ana."

Madison had to laugh. The girl was gripping her banana so tightly she was smooshing it. Her navy-blue Keds had holes in the toes, and her toenails were painted pink. Madison didn't reply; she just motioned with her head, letting the new kid with the missing front teeth know she could tag along with her.

Ana took a bite of her banana that was too big for her small mouth and mumbled, "How old are you?"

Madison found her rock again and gave it a good kick. "Eight. How old are you?"

"Seven. What's your name?"

"Madison, but you can call me Maddy."

"Want some banana?"

Madison grimaced at the ripe banana that was oozing out of its skin. "No, thank you. But I'll probably have to call you Ana Banana from now on."

"My name is Ana Margareta Maria Perez."

Due to the missing teeth, Perez came out as *Pereth*, but Madison knew what she was trying to say. "Wow, that's a lot of names. I'm Madison Prescott." She sighed, not wanting to admit her full name. "Madison…George…Prescott."

"That sounds like a boy's name. And why is your hair so white?"

Madison had heard it all before. Towhead is what some people called her because of her white hair. She hated being called that, but her mom said it would darken over time. That had yet to happen. "Yeah," she shrugged. "My last nanny said when I tell a fib, my hair turns white." The other thing Ana said, about Madison having a boy's name, well, that was true. "My mom said I got two boy's names 'cause that's how bad my dad wanted a boy. Beats me what's so great about boys."

"Yeah, beats me too." Ana shrugged. "And my mom says if I tell a fib, my eyesight will get really bad, and I'll have to get glasses."

Madison stopped short. "Really?"

"Yeah, really."

"I'm so doomed," Madison whispered. She'd be blind by the time she turned ten; she just knew it. She'd need to see about gluing her broken glasses back together.

"I like your names," Ana said.

"You do?" That surprised Madison. Most people weren't shy about informing her that her name should be Mary or Margaret or some other M name. Anything but Madison. No other girl in her whole school shared her name.

Ana finished her banana and stuffed the peel into her front pocket. "Hey, can I kick your rock?"

Madison gave her a nod. It wouldn't hurt to see what this little girl was made of. She folded her arms and waited as Ana geared herself up to give the rock a good whack. It hit the iron gate with a loud clang. "Not bad for a pipsqueak."

Ana turned around and covered her ears and then her mouth. Shoot, was she going to cry? Madison draped her arm over her shoulder and turned them back toward the house before any tears could fall. "Don't sweat it. It's just a gate. And that's quite a leg you got there. You should play soccer."

"I should?" Ana glanced back at the gate. "Don't tell my mom I did that. She'll be so mad."

Madison patted her shoulder. "Stick with me, kid. I'll show you how the world works." She'd also show her the huge bruise on her butt when the time was right. She was sure Ana would give her the reaction she wanted—a total gross-out face.

"You sound like a grown-up," Ana said, looking up at her.

"Yeah." Madison had heard that before too. She'd gone through a few nannies who complained that she was "precocious" and "mouthy." Whatever. They were just mad because she could out-talk them.

"Maybe we could play soccer in this park," Ana said. "Except, I don't have a ball."

Madison giggled. "This isn't a park, silly. This is my lawn."

Ana scrunched her nose as she scanned the property from left to right. "Isn't it for everyone? Like, the people who live in that apartment building?"

Silly kid. Madison just shook her head and smiled. "That's my house."

"Wow." Ana looked up at the mansion in disbelief. "You must have a huge family."

"Nope. Just me and my dad."

"Oh." Ana seemed to accept the explanation. "Well, do you want to come to my new house and play? I have board games."

Madison could've told Ana about the swimming pool and spa around back. She could have mentioned the horse stables that were just down the hill. And the putting green on the other side of the house. And her new set of golf clubs that were just her size. And all the toys she had, like the croquet set and the tennis rackets. Oh yeah, and the tennis court that lit up at night. She decided to slowly reveal them to her new friend. Maybe surprise her with something new every day. That could be fun. And having a friend who actually lived on the estate would be a dream come true. Bernard, her dad's driver, was an okay tennis player, but who wanted to play with a grandpa all the time?

"I like board games, but I'll probably beat you." She gave Ana's shoulder a light slug. "Just kidding, Ana Banana. Let's go!"

They ran toward the staff quarters, Madison holding back slightly so Ana could keep up. Then, she pulled Ana by the hand to the back of the building. "Wanna see something gross?" She didn't wait for Ana to answer. She pushed her shorts down and slowly moved her underwear out of the way, keeping a close watch for her new friend's reaction.

"Oh! That's disgusting!" Ana covered her eyes with both hands. Madison had to lean against the wall she was laughing so hard. Yeah, this would work out just fine.

CHAPTER THREE

Madison downed the last of the bourbon in one gulp. She pushed her empty glass away and clasped her hands together, leaning her elbows on her father's desk. It was all hers now, including this library that smelled like old leather, cigars, and the spicy cologne her father had worn for years.

The walls were covered with portraits of her predecessors. Every Prescott man since the early 1800s had sat for a painting. They were all there, looking down on her. George in his three-piece suit with a Cuban cigar poking out of his breast pocket instead of a handkerchief.

She too would have her portrait painted when she turned forty. George was an enigma in that way. A misogynistic pig through and through, except when it came to Madison. His blood ran through her veins, and somehow, that gave her a free pass that the other Prescott women hadn't been given. She'd been *allowed* to go to Yale. *Allowed* to enter the business world. She just had to do it all on George's terms.

The appointment had already been set for the sitting. If the same artist who had painted her father's portrait was still alive four years from now, he would also paint Madison. She was told to wear navy blue, just like her father and his father before that. A suit, not a dress. And no jewelry. Her hair was to be pulled back in a bun. That part was fine. She wore her hair in a long, straight style anyway, hitting just below her shoulders. It was long enough for a bun, though she never wore it that way.

The part that bothered her was the no jewelry rule. It wasn't a rule in real life, so why for the portrait? Her great-grandfather wore a pocket watch that now belonged to her. Another heirloom she'd been entrusted to pass on to the next generation.

Her grandfather wore a pearl pin in his tie. She looked closely at every portrait, and they all had some sort of adornment. All of them except George. His only adornment was a goddamned cigar.

So, it was just George making yet another decision on Madison's behalf. Well, fuck him. He was six feet under. Quite literally, thanks to Ana and Madison.

Madison would wear her pearl earrings and necklace for the sitting. She'd wear her Rolex. And she'd wear whatever dress she damn well wanted to wear. Maybe a loud print. Give the library some color. And maybe she'd pull down those heavy, hunter green, velvet drapes while she was at it. Matter of fact, she could just have her dress made out of those godawful drapes. That would certainly be one way to get George turning in his grave. One of many, Madison hoped. She looked around the room and saw her father's humidor sitting on the desk. It could go right now, given a slight push. It hit the floor with a loud crash, and Madison scanned the desk to see what else she could ruin.

She'd suffered so many losses in that room. The arguments with her father were always intense. Madison would sit on one side of the desk while her father sat in his big chair, making threats she couldn't possibly overcome. For all the money and power the world thought Madison had, she was helpless as long as George Prescott was alive. Her power was an illusion, and no one really knew it except George. And Madison, of course.

Madison jumped when she heard the door open. Scott poked his head in. "Can I come in?"

Madison took her hand off the crystal paperweight she was just about to throw and waved him into the room. "Just in time for a drink." She went over to the bar and poured them both a bourbon, making hers a double.

He loosened his tie and sat on the leather sofa. "How are you doing?"

Madison shrugged and handed him a drink. She sat at the other end of the sofa with her knees up, facing him. She wrapped her long sweater tighter around her body and kept her eyes on the fire burning in the fireplace. Scott leaned over and rested his hand on her knee. "Is it just the stress?"

"What do you mean?"

Scott reached over and wiped a tear from Madison's cheek. "You haven't cried at all, so I just wondered..."

Madison huffed at the comment. "I can't cry for my father? What kind of unfeeling animal do you think I am?"

"This is me, Maddy. I've known you since you were eighteen. Talk to me."

Madison pulled her sleeve down over her hand and wiped her eyes with it. She could try all she wanted, but there was no stopping the tears. Scott had never let her down. He'd never betrayed her trust, and she would never betray his. She took a deep breath. "After you left. After everyone left, Ana showed up."

"Ana." Scott searched Madison's eyes for answers. "*The...* Ana?"

Was there any other Ana? As much as Madison wanted to drown her sorrows in more bourbon, she knew she'd regret it in the morning. She set the glass down and picked up a bottle of water. "She hates me."

Scott moved in closer and pulled Madison's legs over his. He took off her sock and with a tender touch, rubbed her foot. "I don't want to sound insensitive, but did you really expect her to just forget the past?"

"No." Madison shook her head. "But I didn't expect the hate I saw in her eyes. Not after all this time."

"She went to the funeral. That's something, right?"

That was probably generous. Madison was pretty sure Ana hadn't been at the church for the service. Surely, she would've felt her presence there, just like she'd felt it at the cemetery. "It wasn't like that. She didn't come to pay her respects; she came to spit on his grave. And who can blame her?" Madison wiped her cheeks with her sleeve. "I paid off the groundskeeper to walk away, and we buried him together."

"What?"

"You should've seen her with that shovel. It felt like we'd murdered him and were trying to cover up the evidence. So, as burials go, I'd say it was a pretty good one."

Scott shook his head in disbelief. "You and Ana buried George?" He chuckled as he leaned his head back against the sofa. "God, I wish I could've seen that. I would've helped you."

Madison had thought about asking Scott to stay with her after everyone else had gone, but instead, she'd asked him to see to things at the estate. A lunch had been prepared for the guests, and someone needed to be there.

Scott turned to her. "What does she look like now? I've only ever seen that photo you keep in your drawer. How old were you, sixteen? Seventeen?"

"It was the summer before I went to Yale." Madison pursed her lips together. There were so many things she would do differently given the chance. But would any of it have made a difference as long as George was alive? It was a question that would remain unanswered, and there were days when that reality had been almost too much to take. "Now? She's beautiful," she whispered. "I can't even describe how beautiful."

"Try."

"When we were young…" Madison smiled. "She was my Ana Banana. My little sidekick with long braids that would bounce when she ran. God, we had fun together."

"And now?"

Madison sighed. "Ana Perez, the adult, is stunning. Her hair is short now. It suits her." Her eyes started to tear up again. "And if it weren't for George, she'd be my wife, and we'd have a family and..." Madison remembered who she was talking to. "I'm sorry." She looked down at her water bottle and started picking at the label. "I shouldn't have said that."

"No, it's okay." Scott reached for her hand. "We both knew what we were getting into."

Madison knew she was her "father's daughter." The genes had been passed down, good and bad. Every day, she tried to be a better person than he was, but sometimes, it felt as if she was fighting a losing battle. "I hope you don't hate me as much as Ana does."

"You're exactly who you had to be, Maddy. But there's so much more of you that I get to see that nobody else ever does. You're so beautiful and kind and loving, and you don't have a judgmental bone in your body. Yes, you're damn tough, but you had to be. George wouldn't take anything less from his only heir, and you'll run that company better than any man could. Better than George ever did."

"Scott." Madison gave his hand a gentle squeeze and smiled. "I'd love to say I couldn't have done it without you, but we both know I could have."

Scott laughed. "Well, you are the smartest woman I know. That's why I married you, after all."

"Well, one of the reasons," Madison said with a wink.

They sat in silence for a moment. Madison leaned her head against the sofa and closed her eyes. Only a few seconds had passed before she opened them again and sat up. "I forgot about Aunt Nora."

"She took a sleeping pill," Scott said. "She won't be bothering you anymore tonight."

Madison breathed a sigh of relief. "Thank God. All that wailing at the gravesite was just so nauseating."

"Seriously! Carrying on like Scarlett O'Hara." Scott slid off the couch and fell to his knees. He raised his hands to the heavens and cried out in the worst possible Southern accent, "With God as my witness, I shall never be a penniless social climber who waits thirty years to call on her dying brother again!"

Madison laughed, giving him a good-natured kick in the ribs. "Now I remember why I married you."

"My winning personality and irresistible looks?"

"No. It's because you always find the most appropriate way to comport yourself in a time of mourning."

"That's true." He grinned. "But I can't take all of the credit. I learned everything I know about mourning from Aunt Nora."

Madison didn't know her aunt Nora very well. She'd seen very little of her until six months ago when George had been diagnosed. At first, Madison thought it was sweet when Nora moved into the mansion, insisting on staying in the room right next to her younger brother. She assumed Nora loved George enough to see him through his last days. It didn't take long for her to realize that the insufferable woman was there for one reason only: to claim part of the massive inheritance.

Nora would be furious when she found out that George had left her an insultingly small amount of what should've been their shared inheritance from Madison's grandparents. She still wasn't sure how she was going to tell her aunt the bad news or if she should just give her what was rightfully hers. Then again, what had Nora ever done for Madison? Nothing. Less than nothing.

1994

"You let Madison play with *that* kid?"

George eyed his older sister over his morning paper. All he wanted to do was enjoy his coffee out on the veranda, undisturbed.

That expectation had been shattered when his sister had shown up entirely unannounced two days ago. Two *long* days ago.

George had hoped for an equally sudden departure, but he instead found yet another otherwise pleasant morning interrupted by Nora's incessant need to chirp. One would think that someone who enjoyed hearing her own voice so much would prioritize the development of superior conversational skills. Sadly, this was not the case for Nora Prescott Moretti.

"That kid, Georgie. Why do you let Madison play with that kid?"

He glanced out at the two little girls playing with a soccer ball on the lawn and rolled his eyes. "For God's sake, Nora, what do you want me to do? Tell the school she can't make friends?"

Nora stared at him as if he'd lost his mind. "You can't be serious!"

"Do you have any idea what kind of hell I'd pay for complaining about this?" George gestured toward the two girls. "That school's full of rich liberals. Those assholes love to show the world how diverse McMaster Academy is. Never mind they think diversity is what happens when celebrities bring home babies from their bleeding-heart trips to third world countries."

Nora stiffened in her chair and patted her perfectly coiffed hair. "Dear brother, do you seriously not know who that child's mother is?"

George sighed heavily. "As it happens, Madison hasn't been able to keep a nanny since her mother died, and that little shit seems to be keeping her out of my hair." George folded his paper and dug into his scrambled eggs, hoping the conversation would soon be over. He had a ten o'clock tee time, and his sister's unexpected arrival was damn sure not going to get in the way of that.

❖

Nora's patience with her half-wit brother had run thin. Just because there was no longer a woman in the house didn't mean they should all turn into heathens. She smoothed out her skirt and picked up her cup of tea, holding it delicately, the way a woman of her social status should.

Maybe she shouldn't have moved to Italy when she did. They'd lost both parents, and George had lost his wife, all while Nora was an ocean away.

The cold hard truth was, she had nothing left to talk about with her brother. The only side of George Prescott that Nora knew was this side. Cold, gruff, self-serving George. He'd been that way since birth, as if he somehow knew he'd been born into American royalty and also that his older sister would have claim to nothing that he didn't generously give to her.

The Prescott fortune, made in the banking industry by their father and grandfather, was left solely to George thanks to their misogynistic father who firmly believed women were only good for one thing. Luckily, Nora was smart enough to marry into money. She didn't need the mansion she'd grown up in. George could have it for all she cared. But she'd be damned if her own son wouldn't get what was coming to him.

George didn't have a male heir, and Nora couldn't for the life of her see the little freckle-faced tomboy, who had been standing on her head for at least a full minute while that little girl egged her on, inheriting the company along with the family fortune. How could she possibly run a company of that size? Oh, no. Nora would not allow that to happen. "Alfio will be attending Yale this year." A sense of pride washed over her as she said the words, but she held back the toothy grin that so badly wanted to pop out.

George snorted. "Bought his way in, did ya, Nora? He'll have to brush up on his English. Last time I talked to him, he kept speaking that damned Italian."

"He was probably just showing off, George. He speaks French fluently as well." Nora smirked. George couldn't speak anything but his native language, poor guy. "We hope you'll do the right thing and give him a position in the company when he graduates."

George set his fork down and picked up a pack of cigarettes. He took a long drag and glared at his sister while he slowly blew the smoke out. "Don't waste your money on Yale, Nora."

Nora's jaw dropped. "What on earth are you talking about? Yale is the only choice for Alfio. Grandfather, father, and you, George. That's where the Prescott men go. Period."

"True." He took another long drag on his cigarette. "Prescott men. Not Italian ruffians."

Nora slapped the table with her palm. "Take it back, George. You know my husband has nothing to do with the mafia. He's a banker, for God's sake."

"Be that as it may, dear sister, I have an heir." George motioned with his head toward Madison.

Nora could see past the smarmy grin on George's face. He knew it wasn't the best plan. A son would be so much better. If not a son, a nephew, surely.

George ground his cigarette into the ashtray. "Nora, I'd rather give my fortune away to charity than give it to that Italian you married or his awful spawn."

Nora froze. She couldn't lose her temper, or George would call his lawyer right there at the table and cut her off completely. She needed her trust fund. It was smaller than she'd deserved, but she couldn't risk losing it in case her marriage fell apart. Time had taken its toll on her body, and she knew it wouldn't be long before her husband found someone younger than her forty-five years. To be honest, she was surprised it hadn't happened already.

"Perhaps it was premature to bring this up," Nora said, her expression tightening. "We'll continue this conversation at a later date." She stood up and started to leave, but her pettiness got the best of her when she saw Madison drop to the ground, her face bright red from standing on her head for too long. She turned back to her brother, and gesturing at the giggling girls, she said, "I'm sure your little heiress will be adequately prepared to take over the business one day. Surely there's not much her own kind can teach her that she can't learn from your maid's daughter." With a rueful smile, she leaned down and kissed his cheek. "Good to see you, brother."

As Nora walked across the veranda toward the French doors, a grin spread across her face. Her smile grew even wider when she heard the unmistakable bellow of her brother's gruff voice.

"Madison! Come here, right now!"

Madison reluctantly trudged up to her father, her face still pink from standing on her head, grass stains on both knees. "Yes, Daddy?"

George leaned in close and took his daughter's chin in his hand. "You're a Prescott. Repeat it."

"I'm a Prescott."

"I don't play with the damned gardener. Say it."

"Ana's not—" George squeezed his fingers tighter on her chin. "I don't play…with the damned gardener."

George leaned back in his chair. "Good girl."

Nora's smile grew as Madison's eyes filled with tears. She wiped them away and met her aunt's gaze. Nora wagged her finger at Madison, letting her know she was a naughty little girl.

CHAPTER FOUR

Carmen let herself into her daughter's apartment and picked up the trail of dirty clothes that were still on the floor. She threw Ana's bra and underwear in the clothes hamper and put the skirt and blouse in the dry-cleaning bag. The shoes would take some work to get clean. She set them in the bathroom sink.

"Mom, what are you doing?"

Carmen stood at the foot of her daughter's bed. Ana's arm was flopped over her face. "You ride a horse every Saturday for eight years, and you think I won't worry when you take a day off? I know when something's wrong, my love." She motioned with her hand toward the clothes hamper. "And now, you can get out of bed and explain to me why you decided to plant green beans in your Sunday best."

Ana sat up in bed. "You know those are my work clothes. And are you really going to bring up the green beans again?"

"You were so sweet, wanting to plant green beans for all of the poor, hungry children in the world."

Ana rolled her eyes. "I was six years old."

Carmen chuckled as she turned to leave the room. "Get up. It's after ten. I'll make breakfast, and then you can tell me about these clothes."

"I went to the funeral yesterday."

Carmen stopped in her tracks and turned back around. She'd seen it in the paper, that George Prescott had passed away, but it never occurred to her that Ana would want to attend his funeral. She took a few steps closer. "Did you see her?"

Ana nodded. "I just wanted to watch them put him in the ground. I wanted to watch them bury the son of a bitch with that backhoe. But then, a strange thing happened."

"What? What happened?" Carmen could see the distress on her daughter's face. That combined with the dirty clothes lying in the laundry had her worried. It was the only thing that kept her from chastising her daughter for such unladylike language.

"Madison was there, all alone," Ana said. "Once the casket had been lowered into the ground, she paid the groundskeeper to walk away. And then…" Ana paused and ran her fingers through her messy hair.

"And then what?" Carmen didn't like this story. What in the world had happened at that cemetery?

"And then, Madison took off her gloves and coat."

Carmen covered her hand with her mouth.

"That's when I got out of the car." Ana opened her hand and ran her finger over the blister. "There were two shovels. I helped bury him."

Carmen sat on the bed, shocked by what she'd just heard. "Madison buried her own father? With you?" She shook her head in disbelief. "I suppose as long as the priest did the committal…"

"Seriously? Don't you think George will have a bit more to answer for than that?"

"That isn't for you to decide, my love. And I guess I shouldn't be surprised by Madison's behavior. Mr. Prescott never did do anything for that girl."

1993

Carmen hummed a tune as she dusted the large paintings in the hallway of the second floor. She often spoke to her mother in soft whispers as she worked, telling her all about the life she was living in America and bragging about her only child. "You would be so proud of her, Mama. In English, they say 'she's smart as a whip.'"

Carmen always spoke in English unless she was praying. She knew Ana wouldn't learn Spanish if she didn't speak it in the home, but she didn't care. Ana was American. She had no need for her mother's native language.

Carmen worked hard to be fluent in English. She watched and listened and learned from everyone she spoke to. It was one of the reasons she had been chosen to work on the Prescott estate. Mr. Prescott wanted fluent speakers, she'd been told. And fluent she was, even though she still had an accent.

After working on the estate for a year, Carmen felt as if she and Ana had finally found a real home in Connecticut. The public school was good and so was the library where they spent most Saturday mornings. There were wide open spaces for her to play in and rolling green hills everywhere you looked. Their tummies were full. They were settled. They were safe. And Carmen felt very blessed.

The mansion she worked in was gigantic. It took four of them just to keep it clean. On Mondays, she tackled the nine bathrooms. Most were rarely used, but that didn't matter. They cleaned them anyway.

On Tuesdays, she polished furniture. Because the Prescott's had the kind of furniture that wasn't just dusted. It was polished. Wednesdays were spent changing and washing linens that were mostly clean.

But this was a Thursday, and Thursdays were for cleaning things regular people didn't even know got dirty. Carmen climbed up a ladder to dust off the frame of a massive oil painting, taking great care to avoid touching the painting itself. She stopped when she heard a noise. She listened intently for a moment, then climbed back down the ladder. She took a few hesitant steps toward Madison's bedroom, which Carmen felt was much too far away from her father's bedroom, but that wasn't any of her business.

The door was ajar, and through the crack, Carmen could see the little girl curled up in a ball on her bed, crying. "Miss Madison?" Carmen pushed the door open a few inches.

Madison looked up through tear-filled eyes, her little cheeks red and tear stained. She stopped crying but still convulsed, trying to hold back her sobs. "Yes?"

Carmen took a few steps into the room. "Miss Madison, what's wrong? Can I help?" That's when she noticed the picture frame Madison gripped with both hands. She'd been told that Mrs. Prescott had passed away a year before she'd been hired, making it two years now that Madison had been without a mother. She sat down on the edge of the bed and without hesitation, Madison fell into her arms.

Carmen froze at first, not sure how it would look to the other staff or even Mr. Prescott if he were to walk in. With a cautious touch, she wrapped her arms around the little girl and tried to comfort her. "Shh, it's okay little one."

Carmen spoke in a hushed tone as she ran her fingers through straw-colored hair. "Sometimes, when we miss someone so much it feels like we're going to die without them, it helps to talk to them, even though they aren't here. That's what I do while I'm working. I talk to my mother every day."

Madison wiped the tears from her eyes and looked up at Carmen. "Is your mom dead like mine?"

Carmen shook her head. "No, I don't think so. But I can't ever go back to Mexico and visit her, so it feels like she's gone from this world." Carmen tried to smile. "But she's always with me, if that makes any sense."

"Yeah. Kinda." Madison snuggled in a little closer and wiped her nose with the back of her hand. "But Daddy says I should forget about her because she's gone, and she's never coming back."

Carmen held back a gasp. How could a father be so cruel to his only child? She wanted to tell Madison that her mother was in heaven, watching over her and to never ever forget her. Memories are *everything*, she wanted to say. But she couldn't say any of it, for fear little Madison would repeat her words, and she'd lose her job. She had a daughter to take care of. Her own daughter had to be her first priority. There still had to be a way to comfort little Madison. "What color was your mother's hair?"

Madison tapped her own head. "Blond. Like mine."

"And what color were her eyes?"

"Um…" Madison took a second to think about it. "Brown! I have my Daddy's blue eyes."

Carmen smiled. "Good. Now, it doesn't matter where she is, just like it doesn't matter where my mother is. We can still talk to them when we're feeling sad. And if you ever feel like crying again, come and find me because I don't want you to cry alone, okay?"

Madison nodded and wiped her nose across her sleeve. "Don't tell Ana you saw me crying, okay?"

Carmen pulled her closer, hugging her tightly. "My darling, Ana knows what it's like to lose a parent. She was too little to remember her father, but she still misses him. Maybe you could tell her all the wonderful things about your mother, and she can tell you what she's learned about her father." She lifted Madison's chin so they were eye to eye. "It's good to talk about what makes us sad. Don't keep it inside, okay?"

"Okay." Madison wrapped her arm around Carmen's waist. "I wish you were my nanny."

Carmen almost laughed at the absurdity of it. Everyone knew Mr. Prescott required a certain type of woman to be his daughter's nanny. A rigid, orderly woman, to be precise. One without a motherly bone in her body, from what Carmen had witnessed.

She took a tissue out of her pocket and had Madison stand up in front of her. She wiped her tears away and had her blow her nose. "I can't be your nanny, but we can be secret friends. Every time we see each other, we'll wink. Can you wink?"

Madison tried to wink but ended up closing both eyes. They winked back and forth to each other, making Madison giggle. Carmen straightened Madison's sweater over her school uniform and patted her cheek. "I think I saw some chocolate milk in the fridge. Would you like some?"

Madison grinned and took her hand. "That's my favorite."

Present Day

Ana's mom filled a coffee cup and sat down at the table. "What did Madison have to say for herself?"

"Nothing." Ana took a sip of the hot drink. "I didn't stay. We didn't talk. We shoveled dirt on him in silence."

"You just took it upon yourself to help someone you haven't seen in fifteen years?"

"Not just someone. Madison, Mom. And it wasn't her I was helping."

"That's what I'm concerned about, Ana. Why would you do that?"

Ana kept her eyes on her hands. She ran her fingers over rough spots that would surely turn into callouses. Maybe that was okay. They'd be a good reminder of what she'd done. And she could keep her mind off of just how much it hurt to hear Madison's voice again. "That's not the worst of it." She took another sip of coffee and held on to the cup in an effort to keep her hands from shaking. "I spit on his grave."

Ana's mom gasped. "You..." She made the sign of the cross and clasped her hands together. "Ana."

"It's okay, Mom. Lightning isn't going to come down and strike me dead."

"How do you know? You shouldn't have done that."

"I know. But what's done is done. Isn't that what you always say?"

"Yes." She grabbed Ana's hand. "You must move on from the past now. You've never been able to put that part of your life behind you, but it's time, Ana. Look at what a beautiful life you have! You have all the money you could need. You have a beautiful woman who will love and cherish you if you'd let her!" Ana tried to pull her hand away, but her mom held on tight. "No, Ana. You will listen to me carefully." She waited until Ana had acquiesced with a nod. "Bury them both. In your heart, bury Madison. Spit on her grave if you have to. Spit on everything she did to you and move on. Do you hear me? Move on, Ana. Before your life has passed you by."

Ana wiped away the tears that had welled up in her eyes. She would move on. She had to. But that didn't change the fact that she found herself wishing she could've found even just one kind word for Madison. She'd stood there, crying by her father's grave, and all Ana could do was watch. Had she really become so callous? So hollow? So shut down?

Yes, it was time to move on. Because even though Ana had driven herself hard to get where she was—a career on Wall Street that anyone would envy—she'd never allowed herself to really love again. Not like Madison. Not anything like the way she'd loved Madison. She couldn't.

2002

Ana looked around their small apartment in the staff quarters and wondered if her mother hadn't been right about celebrating her seventeenth birthday at the pizza place in town. Her friends didn't seem to mind that it was a tight fit. They were too busy chowing down on the take-out pizza and canned soda her mother had splurged on.

Her mom made her way to Ana through the crowd of kids. She cupped her cheeks and rubbed their noses together as she'd always done. "I'm so proud of you, Ana Banana. Happy birthday."

Ana blushed. Even her own mom used Madison's nickname for her. Luckily, she hadn't said it loud enough for her friends to hear. "Thank you, Mom. It's wonderful." She whipped her head around when the front door opened, hoping it was Madison.

"Ana, it's for you." Her friend waved Mr. Prescott's driver into the apartment, but he chose to stay on the porch.

Ana stepped out onto the porch with him. Bernard was a nice man who wore the same thing every day: a black suit and tie. Like some of the other staff, he had been a constant presence in her life over the last ten years. Ana had no family other than her mother, so she liked thinking of Bernard as a grandfather. He was kind and had a reassuring voice like she imagined a grandfather would.

Bernard bowed as if Ana were royalty and presented her with a small box. "For the birthday girl."

Her mom walked up behind her. "Hello, Bernard." She looked at the small velvet box and gasped. "Oh, my!"

"It's from all of the staff," Bernard said.

Ana looked to her mom for permission to open the box. She gave her a nod. "Open it."

"Oh, Bernard!" Ana ran her finger over the gold star hanging from a delicate chain.

"We wanted you to know how very proud we are of you, Ana. We know you've earned straight A's four years running, and your birthday seemed as good a time as any to celebrate the accomplishment."

Ana reached up and wrapped her arms around his neck. "Thank you, Bernard. I'll thank everyone else later."

Bernard gave her a pat on the cheek. "Don't you worry about that. Have fun with your friends."

He turned to leave but stopped when Ana said, "Bernard, have you seen Maddy?"

Ana's mom and Bernard exchanged a look. She put her hands on Ana's shoulders. "Honey, I'm sure Madison has other things to do tonight. Good night, Bernard. And thank you for giving Ana such a beautiful gift."

"Good night." Bernard gave Ana a wink and left.

Her mom wrapped her arms around Ana from behind. "I don't think she's coming, sweetheart. You know it's hard for her to get away sometimes. Please don't let it ruin your night, okay?"

"Yeah. I guess not." Ana made every effort to look as if it didn't bother her. She knew she wasn't succeeding, but she smiled and handed the jewelry box to her mother anyway. "Will you put this on me?"

❖

When the festivities were long over and Ana was in bed, she heard a light knock on the door. She sat up and looked over at her mother sleeping in the twin bed on the other side of the room. "Ten minutes," her mom mumbled.

Ana jumped out of bed and threw a robe on over her nightshirt. She opened the door, and her heart skipped a beat. Madison stood there, smiling that crooked smile of hers, holding a small present in both hands. "Sorry I'm late."

Ana pulled Madison into the apartment and wrapped her arms around her neck. Madison giggled as she wrapped her hands around Ana's waist and lifted her off the ground, spinning her in a circle. "Happy Birthday, Ana Banana. How does it feel to be seventeen?"

"I'm only one year younger than you again, and my curfew is an hour later," Ana said, excitement filling her voice. "What took you so long?"

Madison shrugged. "You know *George*. Always cramping my style." She held out the small rectangular box with a big white bow on it. "I come bearing gifts."

Ana took the gift and Madison's hand, pulling her to the sofa. "Is it my own Nokia phone?"

"No. You can blame your mom for that one."

Ana's mom came out of the bedroom in her robe and slippers; her long, dark hair that was usually pulled back into a tight braid flowed freely on her shoulders. "Not until she's eighteen." She gave a slight nod and went to the fridge. "Hello, Miss Madison."

"Hello, Mrs. Perez."

"Why is it that I'm Carmen in the big house, but I'm Mrs. Perez here?"

"Because this is your house," Madison said. "And you're older than me."

"And also because you want to stay on my good side, hmm?" Ana's mom poured herself a glass of milk and got a few cookies out of the cookie jar. As she headed back into the bedroom, she stopped in front of Ana and gave her a kiss on the forehead. "One last happy birthday wish, my love." She gave Madison a wink. "Good night, troublemakers. Don't stay up too late."

Ana waited for the bedroom door to shut before she turned back to the gift she had yet to open. "Okay, so it's not a phone, and it's definitely not the pink Izod shirt with matching boat shoes I so badly want."

"When did you get so preppy?" Madison poked Ana's side, making her yelp. "Shh, just open it," she whispered.

Ana tugged on the white silk bow. She couldn't imagine what was inside the small box. It felt too heavy to be jewelry. Whatever it was, she would surely cherish it since it was from Madison. She took the paper off and read the label. "*J'Adore* by Dior."

"I took one whiff and knew it was perfect for my Ana Banana," Madison said.

Ana's heart skipped a beat. She ran her finger over the gold-embossed word. "What does *J'Adore* mean," she asked, barely above a whisper.

Madison didn't answer immediately, so Ana tore her eyes from the box and risked a look. Madison was smiling at her. "You're in your third year of French, Ana. Why don't you tell me what it means?"

Ana's throat went dry. "I was hoping you'd translate it for me." For months now, she so badly wanted to tell Madison how much she loved her, but every time she tried, she would choke on the words. How did you tell your best friend, who was also a girl, that you wanted to hold her hand and go on dates with her and maybe even kiss her?

You didn't, Ana had decided, seemingly right alongside the rest of the world. You kept it to yourself and never spoke of such things, as her mom would say.

Madison took the bottle out of the box. "Well, I think it means, 'I really wanted a pink Izod shirt and matching boat shoes, not this ridiculously overpriced bottle of perfume.'"

Ana grabbed the bottle, pressing it to her chest. "You're a dork. And I love my new perfume."

"I'd hoped you would." Madison reached over and pushed Ana's long brown hair off her shoulder. "Can I braid your hair?"

Ana didn't hesitate. She slid to the floor and sat in front of her best friend. "Maddy?"

"Yes, Banana?"

"When I turn eighteen, will you stop calling me Banana?"

"I'll stop right now if you don't like it."

"It's not that I don't like it…and that's not what I was going to ask anyway. I was going to ask why you like braiding my hair so much."

Madison chuckled as she split Ana's hair into three sections. "I've been braiding your hair since we were kids. It looks better when I do it, don't you think?"

"I guess." Ana watched the goosebumps pop up on her arms the way they always did when Madison touched her. "Why didn't you come to the party?"

Ana already knew the answer. They'd been hiding their friendship for years. That's why she wanted to have the party at home, thinking Madison could sneak away from the big house and at least watch her blow out her candles.

They had their special hiding places on the estate. Places they could do homework together without getting caught. Places where they could lie down, look up at the sky, and talk about nothing and everything.

They even had a special place where they could leave notes for one another. A piece of mortar had fallen out between two bricks on the privacy wall that flanked both sides of the security gate. Ana checked that spot every day after school. If there was a note, she'd quickly rip a page out of her notebook and write back, tucking the note between the bricks. She'd kept every single one of those notes hidden in a box under her bed. Lately, Madison had been signing those notes with a little heart next to her name instead of her signature winking smiley face. Ana had wondered what that meant. Probably nothing, she'd convinced herself.

Madison stopped braiding and wrapped her arm around Ana, getting close enough to whisper in her ear. "My dad was in a mood tonight. I didn't dare leave until he'd passed out. Good thing for bourbon, right?"

Ana reached up and touched Madison's hand. "I'm sorry, Maddy."

"And I'm sorry I missed your party, but I like this better— just you and me." She let go and finished the braid, then squeezed Ana's shoulders. "Open your present already."

Ana was so mesmerized by Madison's voice in her ear and her fingers running through her hair, she'd forgotten what she was doing, let alone talking about. She opened the box, pulled the lid off the bottle and inhaled. "Mmm. I think I'll wear this for the rest of my life." She dabbed some behind each ear and tilted her head. "What do you think?"

Madison leaned down and inhaled near Ana's ear. "Mmm... perfect."

Ana tried to ignore the goosebumps and got up on her knees. She turned around so they were face-to-face. "What am I going to do without you?" Time was running out for them. Madison would be going off to Yale in a few weeks, leaving Ana at home to finish her last year at the local high school.

Madison spotted the necklace hanging from Ana's neck. She reached out and took the gold star in her hand. "This is pretty. Did a cute boy give it to you?"

"If you call Bernard cute. And stop changing the subject!"

Madison crossed her arms and rested them on her knees. "He's right, you know. You're already a star."

Ana rolled her eyes and groaned.

"Okay." Madison put her hand on Ana's shoulder. "I know you're worried about me leaving, but I promise you, it'll be fine. And you know how I know that?"

"How?"

"Because I don't want to lose you, either."

Ana tried to blink back her tears. It wouldn't ever be the same, and nothing Madison said would change that. But Ana had some things to say too. She took a breath and tried to keep her emotions at bay. "You'll call me every weekend. Friday night if you don't have a date or Saturday morning if you do." It wasn't a request; it was a demand, and Ana blushed at her own bravado.

Madison smiled. "Okay. And since when do I go out on dates anyway?"

"I don't know, Maddy. Since whenever. Just swear it to me," Ana begged.

Madison's expression sobered. She lowered her eyes and stared at her clenched fist. "I didn't want to go to that stupid prom. My dad made me."

"I know. You said he was a total dork." Ana noticed Madison's tightly clenched fist. "What are you hiding?"

Madison's cheeks flushed. "Just...something." She tried to shove her hand in her pocket, but Ana grabbed it. "Ana..." Madison shook her head.

"Another present?" Ana whispered.

"Sort of, but..." Madison studied Ana's eyes for a moment and then nodded. "Yes. I've been meaning to give it to you, but..." She opened her hand, and written in red ink on her palm, were their initials surrounded by a heart, like you'd see carved into a tree.

Ana couldn't breathe. She tried to take a breath, but her lungs were already full. She leaned in, resting their foreheads together. It all of a sudden felt too warm in the room as Madison's breath mixed with her own. One move and she could be kissing her best friend, but she was too scared to move. Too afraid to reveal her true feelings, even though Madison just had.

Could it be real? Could Madison really love her like that? It was true that neither of them had dated boys much. Ana had zero interest in the dorks at her school, and Madison had always said that the boys at her private school were privileged assholes who thought they could just take whatever they wanted whenever they wanted it.

Ana felt Madison's hands move to her waist. They'd been there before, but it felt different now. For one thing, there was no more air left in the room, and Ana was sure they'd both die like this, with their foreheads smashed together. *Breathe, Ana.*

Madison didn't try to tickle her sides the way she usually did. Her hands were just resting there. But not *just* resting there. Madison's hands gripped Ana as if she never wanted to let go. It felt like the best thing in the world, and Ana didn't want to move for fear they would lose the moment forever. But she wanted more. And it seemed as if only one thing could feel even more right than this.

Ana ran her hands up Madison's arms and locked them behind her head. She imagined that if they ever had the chance to slow dance, this was how she would hold her. But a slow dance wasn't what she wanted most. She wanted what she'd thought about every night for the past few months. But could she do it? Her heart was beating so hard she wondered if Madison could hear it. Their foreheads were still locked together, and Ana could barely breathe, but she closed her eyes and let her lips land on Madison's.

And nothing in Ana's world would ever be the same.

CHAPTER FIVE

Jocelyn steeled herself. She'd get scolded for interrupting the sales meeting, but she just might get fired if she didn't. There was no winning. She knew the Perez name, even if Madison wasn't aware that she knew. And she knew enough to interrupt the damned meeting.

When you worked closely with someone for years on end, you learned things. Jocelyn had been Madison's executive assistant for going on eight years now, and while her boss didn't share much about her personal life, there were unintentional divulgences. The old photograph that never left Madison's desk drawer being one of them.

It was always there, sitting loose in the top drawer next to her favorite pens: two teenage girls with their arms loosely wrapped around each other's shoulders, their heads touching. The girl on the left was obviously a younger Madison with her hair bleached out from the sun and freckles covering her nose and cheeks. The other, a beautiful girl with long, brown hair. Jocelyn had touched the photo once, turning it over to see if anything was written on the back. What she found, surprised her.

"Madison G. Prescott

&

Ana M.M. Perez

=

Forever"

At first, she thought nothing of it, thinking it was just a sweet photo of two high school friends. It was only when she'd walked in on Madison staring at the photo with tears rolling down her cheeks on Valentine's Day six years ago that she'd thought twice about the "friends" thing.

And then, there was the conversation she'd witnessed a couple of years ago between Madison and her father.

"How many men do you think that maid's daughter slept with to get that new job of hers?"

Jocelyn swung her head around to the door. She had been going through paperwork with Madison when Mr. Prescott barged his way into his daughter's office. Again.

"Dad," Madison said through gritted teeth. "I'm sorry, Jocelyn. That was uncalled for."

Mr. Prescott waved off the comment with the newspaper he was holding. "Jocelyn's been here forever. She knows how I talk."

"That doesn't make it right. Now, if you don't mind, Dad, we're a little busy. The gala is this weekend."

Mr. Prescott slapped the paper down on Madison's desk. "She's been trying to sleep her way to the top since—"

Madison flew out of her chair. "Don't you dare! I've done my part, George. Say one more word..."

Jocelyn sat there, slack-jawed. Mr. Prescott and his daughter stared each other down, looking like they were two seconds away from ripping each other apart. It was Mr. Prescott who broke the stare first. He glanced at Jocelyn and then back at his daughter. "Not everything, Madison. I still don't have an heir." He turned to leave, and as he walked out of the office, he shouted over his shoulder. "Make it a boy, would you?"

Madison's eyes were locked on the door her father had just gone through. Her chest was heaving, and her eyes were so full of fury, Jocelyn felt the need to break the spell by getting in her line of sight. "Madison?"

Madison held Jocelyn's stare for a few seconds before she sat back down. She looked at the newspaper, then turned it over and forced a tight smile. "I'm sorry, Jocelyn. You've been subjected to my father's rude behavior far too often."

Jocelyn held up her hand. "Not your fault." She picked up her files, knowing they wouldn't get anything else done that day. "We can finish this up tomorrow." Walking as quickly as she could, she made her way to the lobby and found the Wall Street Journal *sitting on a table in the waiting room. She turned to the page Mr. Prescott had been going on about, and there was that name again.*

Ana Perez was the new Senior VP at Danforth Financial. The youngest VP in the history of the company and also the first woman. And not just any woman. A woman of color. She folded the paper back up and tucked it under her arm as she walked back to her desk feeling thrilled that this particular bit of news had gotten under the old man's skin.

So yes, Jocelyn knew things. She steeled herself for whatever was about to happen and opened the conference room door. "Ms. Prescott, Carmen Perez is here to see you. She said you'd know why."

Madison looked up from her paperwork. A dozen sets of eyes turned to her as she seemed to absorb the information in slow motion. "Did you say…"

"Yes," Jocelyn said. "Carmen Perez." She assumed it was Ana's mother, the maid Mr. Prescott had spoken about a few years ago. She seemed the right age, and though she wore a dress, Carmen Perez lacked the stuffy business attire most of their visitors wore.

Madison glanced around the room and then nodded. "Okay," she said, though it was barely audible.

Jocelyn furrowed her brow, confused by the reply. She'd expected a glare followed by a terse reply. She knew Madison was under a tremendous amount of pressure since her father had passed away several weeks ago, so she tried not to take it personally every time Madison snapped at her. "Should I have her wait in your office, ma'am?"

"Yes," Madison said, shuffling papers around, but Jocelyn could tell she wasn't really putting them in any kind of order. "Yes, I'll meet her in my office."

"Very good, Ms. Prescott." Jocelyn closed the door and went back out into the waiting room, smiling as she walked up to Mrs. Perez. "If you'll please follow me." She wanted to be friendly if this really was who she thought it was, so she slowed down and walked next to the woman. "How are you today, Mrs. Perez?"

"I'm fine, thank you."

Mrs. Perez was a thin woman with black hair that she pulled back into a long braid. Her fingers were somewhat disfigured from what Jocelyn assumed was arthritis. She had warm eyes when she smiled. Jocelyn smiled back and held the door open, letting Mrs. Perez walk into the office first. "Ms. Prescott should be here shortly. Is there anything I can get you? A soda or a coffee?"

"I'm fine, thank you." Mrs. Perez tilted her head and smiled. "Your red hair is lovely."

Jocelyn ran her hand over her wavy hair. It had always been her most prominent feature. All of the childhood nicknames had been some derivation of red or orange. It was only when she'd entered adulthood that she'd realized it wasn't such a bad thing. "Thank you, Mrs. Perez." She stood there for a moment and then said, "Okay, then." She wasn't sure what else to say, but she wanted to make sure Madison's guest felt welcome. If this was someone George Prescott had treated poorly, Jocelyn was determined to treat her like a queen. "I'll be right outside if you need anything."

❖

Carmen didn't sit down when the door closed. She wandered around the massive office, looking at photographs that were hung on the wall and strewn about the L-shaped desk. It was hard to believe the woman in the photos was the same girl her daughter had once loved. Madison with President Obama. Madison playing golf with someone who looked famous, but Carmen couldn't quite place the name. Madison standing next to Beyoncé.

Carmen picked up one of the photos and looked at it closely. The little girl with a quick mind and perpetually bruised knees had grown up to be a stunning woman. "Too bad," Carmen whispered as she set the picture back down.

The office was much brighter and more modern than Carmen had expected. For some reason, she'd pictured the adult Madison preferring something like her father's office: massive wood furniture and statues of horses and naked women, a never-used yet mysteriously dusted chess set, and a carafe of properly-aged scotch rounding out the pretentious décor. *Was it called a carafe?* Carmen reminisced, remembering in fine detail the mansion she'd worked in for ten years of her life.

Never mind, Madison's office was nothing like that. Clean lines, minimalist furniture, and almost white carpet. Although it felt very cushiony under her feet, Carmen felt glad she wasn't the person who had to keep it clean.

❖

Madison's heels didn't *click-clack* the way they usually did when she walked down the main hallway of their offices. They were slow, careful steps. Jocelyn stood up as she neared. "She's in your office."

Madison rested her hand on Jocelyn's desk to steady herself. She took a deep breath and stared at the door. "No interruptions."

Jocelyn nodded. "Of course." Madison didn't move. Jocelyn added, "She seems like a lovely woman."

Madison laughed under her breath. "Do I look that scared?" Jocelyn shrugged and gave her a gentle smile.

It was a moment of vulnerability Madison didn't normally allow herself to have in the workplace. Appearing afraid of anything or anyone was a sign of weakness, and George Prescott hated seeing weakness in his only child.

Madison knew this wasn't a friendly visit. How could it be, after everything that had happened? She straightened her suit jacket and took a deep breath. "I better get to it, then."

"Yes, ma'am. If you need anything, I'm here."

Madison gave her a tight smile. "You always are, Joss." She opened her office door and shut it behind her. "Mrs. Perez. It's so good to see you."

Mrs. Perez stood tall as she clutched her purse in front of her with both hands. "Is it?"

Madison clasped her hands together to keep them from visibly shaking. She'd always had a friendly rapport with Ana's mother, and even though she'd expected this exact reaction, it still hurt to know how much the woman despised her. She stood a few feet away and said, "What can I do for you, Mrs. Perez?"

The former maid pointed at one of the photos. "That's your handsome husband? What's his name again? Scott something?"

Madison cringed inside. She suspected Mrs. Perez already knew the answer but wanted to hear Madison say it out loud. "Yes. Scott Fairmont."

"The day we found out you were engaged was a painful one in our home. I read it in the paper, but I didn't want Ana to find out that way, so I had to be the one to tell her." She took in a deep breath and shook her head. "Very bad day."

Madison had no idea what to say. In fleeting moments, she had imagined what that day must've been like for Ana, but over the years, she trained herself to think of just about anything else when it came to Ana. She would wonder what Ana had eaten for breakfast or whether she liked that new style of jeans that drove

Madison crazy. And that song—that stupid song—the one that played over and over on the radio. They'd never once heard it together, of course, but Madison had always wondered whether or not it made Ana think of Madison the way it made her think of Ana.

Ana was so deeply embedded in Madison's consciousness that she once had a particularly sweet cantaloupe and absurdly wondered if Ana would like it. She had berated herself at the time. How could she not know if Ana liked cantaloupe?

That had been Madison's life for the last fifteen years.

She had no choice but to step away from the reality of how she had hurt Ana. She once saw a therapist on a talk show call it "compartmentalizing." It had something to do with tucking away the feelings that made it hard to live your life. It was the only way she could ever have said "I do" to someone other than Ana. To wonder how Ana felt would've been more than she could take. Even Madison knew her excuse wasn't worth much in the face of things, but it was the truth.

And now, many long years later, she found herself faced with the subject she had so carefully tucked away: what Ana must have thought when she married Scott Fairmont.

"I'm so...Mrs. Perez," Madison pleaded. "I'm so very sorry."

Mrs. Perez straightened her shoulders. "That's not why I'm here, but I can't say it didn't feel good to tell you that. You have no idea what my Ana went through. What she still goes through. I have to watch my daughter push people away because she can't trust them. That's your cross to bear, Madison Prescott. That's on you."

Madison wanted to scream that it wasn't her fault. None of it was her fault. But that wasn't completely true. She could've done things differently. God, if only she'd done things differently, maybe things wouldn't have gone so wrong.

"Ana came to me after you pulled that stunt with your grandmother's wedding ring," Mrs. Perez said. "She was so happy, but I should have known better." She gripped her own blouse. "I knew in my heart it was wrong. Why didn't I steer her in the right direction?"

"You would have steered her away from happiness just because she was in love with a woman?"

Mrs. Perez scoffed. "No. My daughter is proud of who she is and so am I. What I regret, and where I failed as a mother, is that I didn't steer her away from *you*!"

Madison shook her head. "Mrs. Perez," she whispered.

"No. I get my say. Do you hear me, Madison? I get my say."

Madison had spent a few minutes of every day for the last fifteen years hoping and praying that Ana had found some happiness in her life. Some peace, at the very least. Time and again, Madison had resisted the urge to google Ana, afraid of what she might find. Of course, she knew Ana had advanced professionally—she couldn't exactly avoid reading the business pages. But she had managed to keep herself from finding out if Ana had found someone.

And now, with Ana's mother standing in her office looking so angry, she knew the truth; that peace and happiness had eluded them both. She pulled out a chair. "Please sit, Mrs. Perez." She sat and patted the seat cushion next to her. "Please."

Mrs. Perez sat down but still held her chin high. "Ana has a lovely lady. A doctor. Her name is Kris, and she would marry Ana in a second. They could have a life together, start a family, maybe. I keep telling her it's not too late. And then, you waltz back into her life and expect me to be quiet?" Mrs. Perez pulled a manila envelope from her purse and threw it in Madison's lap. "You think this money will buy me off? Maybe keep me from telling Ana to stay away from you like I should've done all along? Well, you're wrong. I won't stay quiet this time around. You ruined Ana fifteen years ago. You changed how she sees the world. Her eyes are clouded over with mistrust. So, keep your damned money. I'm not for sale."

So, this was why Mrs. Perez stopped by. Madison didn't realize the information had already been mailed out. She thought it would take at least a month to finalize things.

Even though she knew what was inside, she pulled the paperwork out of the envelope and quickly glanced at it, just to make sure. "Mrs. Perez, this isn't a payoff, and I'm pretty sure Ana has no intention of ever seeing me again, anyway."

Mrs. Perez gripped her purse with both hands. "I know your kind. People like you think they can throw a little money at people like me to stay quiet, but I swear on my father's grave—" She covered her mouth for a moment as tears came to her eyes. "I won't let you hurt her again."

Madison reached over and rested her hand on Mrs. Perez's knee. "And I swear to you, this is nothing more than me settling up my father's will. My dad wanted to take care of the staff, those who had been so loyal to our family. Is that so hard to believe?"

"I never knew your mother, God rest her soul." Mrs. Perez made the sign of the cross. "She passed before I started working for your family. But I knew your father, so yes, it is hard to believe. That man would cut off his right arm before he'd freely give one red cent to me or anyone else who worked on that estate. To him, we were nothing more than dirt under his feet."

Madison took her hand away. "Okay, you're right. This was my doing. And I realize that with Ana's success, you don't really need the money, but the others do. They should be able to have some security. I want that for them, but I couldn't leave you out, Mrs. Perez." She tucked the paperwork back in the envelope and handed back. "Please, take it."

Mrs. Perez took the envelope and stared at it for a moment. "I will take it if you make me a promise. One you won't break this time."

Madison knew what it would be. Mrs. Perez didn't even have to say it. "At the cemetery, Ana made it clear where she stands."

"I want to hear it from you." Mrs. Perez turned in her chair so they were face-to-face. "Promise me, Madison. Promise me you'll stay away from my Ana."

Madison lowered her gaze. Could she make that promise? Keep it? And how dare Mrs. Perez even ask that of her? "Do you know who you sound like?" She kept her eyes on her hands while she waited for a reply.

"Maybe your father was right," Mrs. Perez said. "Maybe I was the one who was bad at parenting."

Madison's head shot up. "You don't mean that, Mrs. Perez." Needing space, she stood up and moved a few feet away. She stood with her back turned for a moment, and when she turned back around, her eyes were filled with tears. "He ruined my life," she said through gritted teeth.

Mrs. Perez also stood up. "And you ruined Ana's. Everything she does, every success she's had, working on Wall Street, even her horse—all of it was to prove herself worthy enough for you and your father." Mrs. Perez put a hand to her mouth to cover her quivering lip. "She wanted to be good enough for your world."

Madison took a step toward her. "She's better than any of us. My father may not have known that, but I always did," she said, pointing at her chest.

Mrs. Perez tilted her head. "Really?" She grabbed one of the small photos of Madison and her husband and shoved it at her stomach, forcing Madison to take it. "This photo says otherwise."

Of course, the photo said otherwise. Madison knew that. But she couldn't do anything about the past. She couldn't turn back time. She set the picture down and put the large envelope back in Mrs. Perez's hand. "Several employees got the same stock package. It's the least I could do. It's also far less than he should've done. Please, take it and know that I never meant to hurt anyone."

"You want to clear your conscience, but I won't let you." Mrs. Perez tossed the envelope on the desk. "I spit on your money the same way you spat on my daughter. And I pray you suffer every day with your guilt." She turned for the door.

"Mrs. Perez, wait." Madison pushed a button on her phone, calling Jocelyn into her office. She opened the door just in time to block the exit.

"Yes, ma'am?"

"Joss, please have Stephen drive Mrs. Perez home."

"No," Mrs. Perez said. "I can get home on my own."

Madison sighed. "It must've taken you two hours to get downtown. Stephen is Bernard's nephew. I know how fond you were of Bernard, my father's driver?"

"It'll be dark soon," Jocelyn interjected.

Mrs. Perez eyed them both. "Fine. But only so I can meet Bernard's nephew and tell him what a nice man he has for an uncle."

Madison cringed. "Bernard actually died a few years ago."

"I'm sorry to hear that." Mrs. Perez made the sign of the cross.

"If you'll come with me?" Jocelyn stepped out of the office.

Mrs. Perez gave Madison a final nod and left the office.

CHAPTER SIX

A na couldn't concentrate. She turned off her monitor and rubbed her temples. It didn't ease the pain that had been building behind her eyes. Nothing had, lately. She eyed the decanter of whiskey sitting on a tray with two lowball glasses. It was strictly for clients, but she needed something if she was going to get through this day.

Her peers did it all the time, having a drink at work. But they were men, which meant they could get away with murder. She had to be on top of her game at all times, and that was the problem. She wasn't performing at peak levels.

The funeral had changed everything. She'd been a mess ever since, mired in memories that she'd long pushed away. One drink would help her forget. If nothing else, she'd relax a little and maybe get some work done.

She poured herself two fingers and, closing her eyes, sank back into her chair. The burn of whiskey felt good on her throat, but she never should've closed her eyes. Memories of Madison quickly filled her head.

2007

Ana felt nervous being on the Prescott estate again. She parked her car in front of the garage and breathed a sigh of relief when it was Madison who opened the massive wooden entry door. "Why am I here?" she whispered.

Madison took Ana's hand and pulled her into the house. "Don't worry. My dad's in the city." She held on to the lapels of Ana's pea coat and smiled from ear to ear. "I promise there's a very good reason for you being here."

Ana wanted to kiss Madison right there in the doorway. Just lay one on her girlfriend, almost wishing George were there to see it. She wondered how long they could go on like this, hiding their relationship from the entire world. Madison tried to act as if it was nothing, as if nothing George said or did ever fazed her, but Ana saw through the façade. She knew the second Madison graduated from Yale, which was just a few months away, George would have her working in New York at the family business. Ana didn't really see a future for the two of them, but she couldn't bring herself to say it out loud.

"You're shaking," Madison said, taking Ana's hands. "Let's go outside."

Ana held on to Madison's hand as they walked down the path to their favorite tree. Being outside felt better. Much better. The tree was a large oak with an old wooden bench set against it. You couldn't see the bench from the big house, so the young lovers had often met there in secret, hoping George wouldn't catch them together. They'd sit there for hours, talking about school or doing homework together. Sometimes, Madison would lay her head in Ana's lap and look up at her with those clear blue eyes. Ana never could resist those eyes. One look and she'd melt in Madison's arms. She knew it was a weakness, but there really wasn't anything she could do about it.

As they walked to the bench, Ana wondered when she'd fallen in love with her best friend. Was there an exact moment, or had she always loved her like this? She glanced over at her. Maddy turned to her and smiled. She squeezed Ana's hand and then pulled her closer, wrapping her arm around her waist. "You look like you have something on your mind," Madison said.

Ana slid her hand into Madison's back pocket. "I was just wondering when I fell in love with you. Was it that time you met me at my school and carried my books home for me?"

"When we were twelve?" Madison smiled. "It was only one book. The one you couldn't fit in your backpack."

"I did have a thing for library books, but that doesn't matter. The point is, somewhere along the line, I fell in love with my best friend, who happens to be a girl."

"I'm still a girl," Madison said. "And I hope you're still in love with me."

Ana tugged on Madison's back pocket, stopping their progress down the path. She slid her hands under Madison's coat and around her waist. "I've been busy with school. Hanging on to this scholarship means everything. And I know I haven't been writing to you every day like I used to, but I love you like crazy, Maddy. I always will."

Madison cupped Ana's cheeks. "It was the day we met. That's when you fell in love with me. You couldn't resist my eight-year-old charms."

Ana laughed. "The year you decided to stop washing your hair because it was inconvenient? That's the year you think I fell madly in love with you?"

Madison slapped Ana on the ass and started walking again. "Oh, come on. That phase only lasted two weeks."

"You're right. The sock phase was much worse. And then there was the coffee phase. God, you were a mess."

"I was a motherless child trying to find herself. Coffee was a necessary evil."

Ana took Madison's hand again. "Please tell me that if we ever have children, you won't let them drink coffee when they're ten."

"They won't need to," Madison said. "They'll have us. And we'll love them the way we love each other."

They walked in silence for a minute, taking in the gravity of what had just been said. They'd joked about growing old together, but they'd never been that specific before. Ana had to wipe away a tear, and it didn't go unnoticed.

"I hope our kids have your eyes. I love your big brown eyes," Madison said.

"We can't, Maddy," Ana said, barely above a whisper. "I'm sorry I said that…about having kids."

Madison let go of Ana's hand and sat next to her on the bench. "Why not? Why can't we have everything everyone else has? There are gay people everywhere. Surely, you've met some at Princeton."

It wasn't the world Ana was worried about. She tucked her hands in her coat pockets. If she were touching Maddy, she might not be able to say what needed to be said. It was time they both faced reality. "Your father has plans for you. And those plans don't include me."

Madison took a deep breath. "How many?"

"How many what?"

"How many kids are we going to have?"

Ana shook her head. She didn't want to hurt Madison. She loved her more than life itself. She ran the back of her fingers over Madison's cheek, trying to find words that wouldn't break both of their hearts. "Maddy…"

Madison took Ana's hand and kissed it. "Marry me, Ana."

Ana's eyes widened in shock. "What?"

Madison got down on her knees and pulled a ring out of her pocket. It was the biggest diamond Ana had ever seen. "It was my grandmother's wedding ring, and I want you to have it. So, Ana Margareta Maria Perez, will you please marry me?"

Madison always did this to Ana, making her feel dizzy and weak in the knees. She didn't know what to say. Her mouth opened, but nothing came out. Had Madison Prescott just proposed to her? For real? She felt a tear run down her cheek and Madison wipe it away, but she also felt numb. As if time had stopped. Maybe it had stopped for them so they could have this moment where they pretended that life was full of possibilities and that somewhere out there was a home. Their home. "Four," Ana whispered. "I want four kids. A big family, with lots of love and laughter." She thought if she made the number big enough, Madison would come to her senses.

"Is that a yes?" Madison was staring at her with all the hope in the world in her eyes. "Ana, you have to say yes before I can put this ring on your finger."

God, what could she possibly say except yes? Yes, Madison. Every day, yes. A thousand yeses. But Ana couldn't say it because that would make it real. But she could nod.

"Ana, you have to say it."

Tears streamed down Ana's face. Maybe she was underestimating Madison. Maybe she really was strong enough to stand up to her father. Maybe they both were. And maybe four kids was two or three too many, but they could figure that out later.

"Ana? You're kind of leaving me hanging here."

Ana laughed through her tears. "Yes, Maddy. Yes."

Madison slid the ring on. It was a perfect fit.

❖

Ana pulled the ring out of her jeans pocket and slid it on her finger. She hadn't seen Madison since their engagement day almost a month ago, but they'd talked on the phone almost every night. She'd mostly kept the ring on a chain around her neck, only wearing it on her finger when she was alone in her apartment at school.

If felt good on her finger. It felt right. She would be Madison Prescott's wife one day, if not legally, at least in their hearts. They'd talked about having a small commitment ceremony…the *wedding*, as Madison insisted on calling it. She used the words "wedding" and "marriage" and "wife" despite the complete lack of legal support. She was adamant that they would have everything straight couples had. She'd even talked about having the wedding in a church until Ana pointed out that they were both technically Catholic, and if she wanted everything straight Catholics got, that would include abstaining until the wedding night. That put a quick end to that particular discussion, but Madison was otherwise undeterred. During their last call, she talked excitedly about going on a honeymoon once Ana graduated. Maybe Paris. Neither one of them could think of a more magical place to celebrate their love. And it would be fun to make use of the French she'd been studying for years. Madison talked about their future with such conviction, Ana had actually started to believe it.

Ana knew there was one thing she'd need to do before their dream wedding could ever become reality. She needed to tell her mother, and it was a conversation she wasn't looking forward to.

Ana looked up at her mother's apartment building and took a deep breath. "Here goes nothing."

Her mom greeted her with a kiss on the cheek. "I just made some chamomile tea."

Ana sat at the table, knowing her mother would insist on waiting on her. "Sounds perfect."

"How is school? And what's so important that you couldn't tell me on the phone? Please, don't tell me you're having trouble. The Lord put such a good head on your shoulders, Ana. Please, tell me you're using it."

"It's good, Mom. I'm doing some tutoring on the side now. Ten bucks an hour."

"That's my girl." Her mom set the cups down and kissed Ana's head. "You're such a good girl. You make your mother proud." She sat down, and when Ana brought the cup to her lips, her mom gasped. "Is that…" Her eyes flicked between the ring and Ana's face.

Ana grabbed her hand. "Don't freak out."

"Don't freak out? You're wearing what looks an awful lot like an engagement ring!" Her mom threw her hands in the air. "I didn't even know you were dating someone!"

Ana lowered her gaze.

"You need to start talking, or I'm going to assume all sorts of horrible things. Oh, *Dios mio*, please don't tell me you're in trouble!"

Ana shook her head. "No, Mom. I'm not pregnant. You don't have to worry about that, I promise."

"Then how? Who? Start talking, young lady!"

"It's…Maddy. She asked me to marry her. That's why I'm here."

"Maddy? Madison?" Her mom stiffened. "Madison Prescott?"

"We're still together," Ana said. "I just don't talk about it much. Or not at all, I guess. We have to be careful."

"My darling." Her mom shook her head in confusion. "We tell each other everything. Why would you hide something like this?"

"Because I knew you'd worry."

"You're my only child, so of course, I worry and pray every day for your safety and happiness. It's what mother's do." Her mom folded her arms and lifted her chin. "I won't talk about this anymore until Madison comes to tell me her intentions."

Ana held up her hand and wiggled her fingers. "Mom, doesn't this ring on my finger tell you what her intentions are? It's her grandmother's wedding ring, and she put it on *my* finger."

"A foolish act by a foolish, naïve girl."

"Mom!"

Her mom shook her head. "Don't pretend this is normal, Ana. This is not just another proposal of marriage. And I'm not talking about the gay aspect of it. I'm talking about…well, you know exactly what I'm talking about."

Ana sighed and plopped back into a chair. "You're talking about George Prescott."

Her mom leaned on the table and took her chin, forcing her to look her in the eye. "I'm talking about four years ago, Ana. How can you just pretend that night never happened? How can Madison pretend it never happened?"

2003

George Prescott tossed the glossy 8x10 photos on the desk. "My God, Albert."

George's private investigator and personal bodyguard quickly put the photos back in the folder, making sure the one of Madison and Ana swimming topless together stayed on the bottom of the pile. "I'm sorry, Mr. Prescott. I warned you it was bad."

"I was only gone for three weeks." George lit up his cigar and opened the folder again. "You're telling me all of these were taken in the last three weeks?"

"They didn't know I was still in town. Madison probably assumed I'd gone to Costa Rica with you. Apparently, they tried to make good use of your time away."

George took a good long sip of his whiskey as he mulled over his options. He thought he'd made it clear years ago that Madison wasn't to associate with the help. He wanted to ask Albert to clarify, but he knew what those photos meant. It meant his only child, his *daughter*, was into girls. "Goddamnit," he growled under his breath. "You take care of that little whore, and I'll handle my daughter."

"Take care of her, sir?"

George hated it when he had to spell everything out for Albert. "Let her know in no uncertain terms that if she comes near my daughter again, etcetera, etcetera. Jesus, Albert."

Albert scratched his balding head. "Sir, her mother works on the property. She's a maid."

"I know that! Throw them both out tonight and make it ugly. I want an example made of that money-grubbing whore."

"It's Carmen's daughter, sir."

George didn't need Albert telling him that. Hell, he liked Carmen. She spoke English well, and he never had to tell her anything twice. Everything was always done right the first time when Carmen did it. But it wasn't as if she was irreplaceable, and Albert certainly didn't need to know he even knew who she was. George threw his hand in the air, causing ashes from his cigar to go flying. "I don't give a flying fuck which maid it is! She's a fucking maid, for Christ's sake! And make sure she never works in this town again. And put the word out about that abomination she calls a daughter."

"Yes, sir."

❖

It took Carmen a moment to get her bearings. The clock said it was close to midnight, so why was someone honking their horn over and over? She got up and went to the front door. She was blinded by car lights when she opened it. She put her hands up to shade her eyes, but she couldn't see who was behind the wheel of the truck. Whoever it was revved the engine and laid on the horn.

"Who's there?"

"Pack your fucking bags and throw them in this truck! Right now, Carmen!"

Carmen knew that voice. It was Albert, the hard-drinking man who sometimes lived in the small room off the kitchen. The staff hated him. He'd go in the kitchen late at night and leave a big mess for them to clean up in the morning, never caring if he left food out to spoil. "Mr. Albert, what is the problem?"

"Your daughter!" Albert got out of the truck and slammed the door shut. "She can't just run around this property like she owns the place! Now, get to packin', Carmen, or I'll go in there and start throwing your shit out the door!"

Ana came to the door in her robe. "What's going on?"

Albert scowled at her. "There's the little whore."

"Mr. Albert!" Carmen shouted. "Do not speak about my daughter that way!"

Albert pushed Carmen out of the way and rushed inside her house, grabbing anything he could get his hands on. He had his arms full as he walked past Ana. "This is how you treat your mother? Did you not think of her when you decided to whore yourself around the property?"

Carmen had no idea what was going on, but she would not let this man say one more word to her daughter. She pulled Ana into the bedroom and cupped her cheeks. "Pack your things, Ana. *Fast!*" Ana just stood there, crying. "Ana!" Carmen went to the closet and grabbed a suitcase. She shoved it into Ana's hands. *"Pack!"*

Carmen didn't dare take the time to get dressed. She and Ana left the apartment still dressed in their robes with suitcases in both hands. Some of the other staff members stood at their doors, watching. Albert leaned against his truck, smoking. He'd haphazardly thrown some of their things from the living room and kitchen in the back of his truck. Things that would break easily, like the TV and microwave.

There was screaming coming from the big house. Carmen shot Ana a glare, letting her know she better not even think of running up there. "Just get in the car, Ana."

Albert started his truck and revved the engine again. He rolled the toothpick that was ever present from one side of his mouth to the other. He grinned at Ana and gave her a little wink. *"Adios,* ladies." He drove to the gate and dumped what was in the back of his truck by the road, leaving it for Carmen and Ana to collect.

Carmen drove out of the gate and stopped by the pile. She looked at Ana. "Do you want any of that stuff?"

Ana glanced at the pile, then turned away. "He broke the TV."
Carmen pulled out onto the road, leaving the pile behind.

❖

The following morning, Carmen sat in a chair, waiting for her daughter to wake up. They'd found a motel a few miles out of town, but it was too expensive for them to stay in for an extended period of time. They'd have to find something more permanent and quick.

"I can feel you staring at me," Ana said groggily. She sat up and pulled her knees up to her chest. "Just say it."

"I don't need to. You already know." Carmen stood up and started pacing. "I told you, Ana. Over and over, I told you."

"We love each other, Mom. Maddy loves me."

"Since you were this high," Carmen held her hand to her waist. "You've known that man did not want you around his daughter, and still, you had to push it. You had to send letters to each other and have secret meetings and what, Ana? Now you're having sex together? Is that why I just lost my job?"

Ana covered her eyes. "Mom…"

"No, Ana! You do not get to hide behind your hands. We've lived there for ten years! Where would you like us to live now? We have no family here! We have nothing except what is in that car! Now, tell me why I lost my job!"

Ana uncovered her eyes and sighed. "When Maddy came back home for the summer, she asked me to go steady with her. And then Mr. Prescott went out of town. Someone must've seen us, I guess."

"Ay, *Dios mio*." Carmen sat back down. "Those aren't our people, Ana. You couldn't find someone—anyone—else to fall in love with?"

Carmen went over to the bed and sat next to Ana, pulling her into her arms and kissing her head. "I want you to reach high in this life, Ana. Reach for the stars and be whoever you want to be. And if Madison Prescott sets your world on fire, then I can't tell you not to love her. But her father can. He's a powerful man, and I'm a maid. You can't expect me to stand up to that, and you can't expect Madison to, either. She could lose everything, including her inheritance."

"Maddy doesn't care about money."

"Says the girl who has too much of it." Carmen lifted her daughter's chin so she could look her in the eye. "It wouldn't be fair to make her choose between you and her family. Do you understand that?"

They both jumped when they heard a loud knock on the door. "Ana!"

"It's Maddy." Ana jumped from the bed and opened the door.

Madison stepped inside and met Carmen's glare. "Mrs. Perez. I'm so sorry."

If it hadn't been for Madison's appearance, Carmen would've ripped into her and told her how selfish she was to put their lives, their wellbeing, at risk. And for what? A little sexual experimentation?

But Madison seemed distraught. Her hair was a mess, her clothes were wrinkled, and she had dark circles under her eyes. Maybe neither of them had slept last night.

Madison turned her attention to Ana, taking her hand. "Are you okay? Did he hurt you?"

"No. He didn't hurt me. He just…"

"Threw our things out on the street," Carmen said, anger brewing in her chest "And then threw us out. Like trash."

Madison was still standing in the doorway. "May I come in?"

Carmen gave a wave of her hand. "So long as you didn't bring that brute, Albert, with you."

"I'm pretty sure he's sleeping off a hangover."

Carmen shook her head in disgust and then folded her arms across her body. "So, what now, Madison? Why are you here?

Because it seems to me that the best thing we can do is get as far away from your father as possible. And unfortunately, getting away from your father means getting away from you too."

Madison pulled an envelope from her jean jacket pocket. "It's all I could get my hands on right now, but I'll get more." She put the envelope in Ana's hand and looked at Carmen, "Do you mind if I sit down?"

Carmen waved her over to the bed. Madison looked as if she was about to collapse from fatigue, so how could she say no? Ana and Madison sat on one bed, and Carmen sat on the other. Madison kept hold of Ana's hand and looked Carmen in the eye. "Don't bother looking for a job here. My father is putting out the word."

"So, he's going to ruin my good name in Connecticut?" Carmen looked at her daughter. "Where would you like to live, Ana? The choice is yours. Somewhere warmer? We could go to Florida."

"Actually..." Madison interrupted. "I know a family in New York. A friend of mine at school. They don't know my father or anyone around here, really. They're city people. I could talk to them. Maybe get you an interview?"

"And where would we live? New York is very expensive," Carmen said.

"I'll help as much as I can. I know this is my fault. We should've been more careful."

"No. I'm not taking money from you, Madison. Ana and I will find our own way in this world. We always have. Ana, give the envelope back to her." Carmen stood up. "And this conversation is over." She waited for Ana to do as she was told, then went to the door. "I'll give you two some time to say good-bye."

Carmen paced outside the door. What a mess they were in. Ana had one more year of high school to get through. She was on track to get a scholarship from one of the big universities. Her teachers and guidance counselor loved her. How could they possibly leave Connecticut right now?

How could they not? If Mr. Prescott found out they'd stayed close by, what would he do? Carmen couldn't risk it. Besides, it was unlikely anyone in the area would hire her. They would have to go to New York. And Ana would have to adjust quickly. She would get that scholarship, no matter what. And if it wasn't enough, Carmen would provide the rest. She'd work three jobs if she had to. Whatever it took, that's what she would do.

They were so sweet together, her daughter and Madison. If only others could see Ana the way Madison did. Without labels or class or judgment. Madison saw Ana not as a maid's daughter but as the beautiful person she was. And because Madison saw Ana that way, Ana saw herself that way too.

She stood up and went back to the door, lightly knocking before she walked in. She found the two girls wrapped in each other's arms, both sobbing their eyes out. "Hey," she said. They both turned and looked at her. "What do you say we go get breakfast and talk about this family in New York who might possibly be in need of a maid?" She winked at Madison. "You're buying."

CHAPTER SEVEN

Present Day

"What is this?"

Ana jumped, causing whiskey to spill from the glass she'd been holding tight to her chest. "Shit, Mom!" She put the glass down and leaned forward, trying to brush the liquid off of her blouse. "You can't just walk in on me like that!"

"And you can't just use language like that." Her mom pulled a handkerchief from her purse and offered it to her. "Kyle said you were alone."

Ana waved the handkerchief off and stomped over to the door. She shut and locked it then went to a small closet that held extra work clothing. "He still should've announced you."

"I think he was running off to the bathroom when I showed up. Don't be mad at him." Her mom sat down and eyed the glass. "This job is too much for you. I knew it when you accepted the promotion."

"Don't be so sexist, Mom. You would never say that if I were your son."

"Fine." Her mom sighed. "I have to tell you something."

Ana buttoned up her clean blouse and sat at her desk. "Is everything okay?"

"It's about Madison."

Ana blinked a few times, then picked up the glass and gulped down the rest of the whiskey. She set the glass back down, hiding it behind her monitor. "What about her?"

Her mom recounted what had happened. The large envelope she'd received. Why she refused to keep it. How she told Madison off for thinking she could buy her silence.

"Wait." Ana rubbed her temples. The headache was still there, but she tried to ignore it. "You said it was a stock certificate, right?"

"Yes. For ten thousand dollars."

"Mom, stock certificates don't have values on them. Are you sure it wasn't for ten thousand shares?"

Her mom paused. "I thought..." She shook her head. "Honestly, I don't know now."

Ana turned on her monitor and typed in the stock symbol for Madison's company. Then she grabbed her calculator. "Mom, I think you just threw away 1.5 million dollars."

"You would want me to take it? That surprises me, Ana."

"And you're trying to hide your shock right now. Mom, Madison just gave you 1.5 *million* dollars."

Her mom lowered her gaze. "I didn't look that closely at it." She huffed out a laugh. "Ten thousand was easy to say no to."

Ana tilted her head. "1.5 million, not so much?"

"I thought she was being so cheap. Can you believe I just threw it back at her like it was below me to accept such a pittance?"

They both giggled. "What a fool," her mom whispered.

"My mother is no fool," Ana said. "And I'm sure the offer still stands."

"I may not be a fool, but I am stupidly proud, and you know it. I would never crawl back there on my hands and knees."

Ana smiled. "I know, Mom. Besides, you'd never spend that money on yourself. Now, why don't you let me take you to lunch, and we can talk about everything except the Prescotts, okay?"

"You're buying." Her mom winked. "I'm just a poor fool."

❖

Carmen opened the door but didn't move to let Madison in. "The last time you were standing in that spot, you were about to ask me for my daughter's hand in marriage."

"I'm surprised you never moved closer to Ana's apartment."

"Don't start. I like where I live. I know my neighbors, and they know me. I don't need some fancy place. And Ana is close enough." She moved aside. "Come in, if you must."

The apartment looked much like Madison had remembered it: cozy and clean, everything in its place. The only photos on the walls were of Ana. Several had been added since she'd last been there. Ana's graduation photo from Princeton hung prominently in the middle of her school portraits.

A pang of hurt washed over Madison. She should have been there that day, cheering Ana on as she took her diploma in hand. How different things would be right now if she'd been there on that day and for every other milestone Ana had reached. God, it hurt to think about how much she'd missed.

"I assume you didn't come here to look at everything you missed out on."

Madison held her stomach, hoping the ache would go away. "No," she said, wondering if Carmen had taken up mind reading.

"I'd offer you tea, but I'm hoping you won't be here long enough for that."

Madison turned and faced Carmen. The hate was so evident in her eyes she had to look away. "Mrs. Perez…" She swallowed hard, trying to hold back her emotions. She didn't come here to cry.

Carmen sighed. "Coffee or tea?"

"You don't have to do that."

Carmen went into the small kitchen and put the kettle on. She turned back around and stopped short, her eyes set on the same large envelope sitting on the kitchen table. "That's why you're here?"

Madison took off her coat. "May I sit?"

Carmen gave her a curt nod. "You always did show me respect in my home. It's good to see that hasn't changed."

"I'd like to think I always showed you respect, Mrs. Perez." Madison sat down and leaned back in the chair, crossing her legs.

Carmen furrowed her brow. "Really? That's what you think? How much respect were you showing me when you were fornicating with my daughter behind my back? Using her—"

Madison shot out of the chair. "I loved your daughter! I wanted to give her everything I had! A good life!"

"She didn't need you for that! She was making a good life for herself! But of course, the great Madison Prescott did whatever the hell she wanted, didn't she? Forget about the consequences! Forget about keeping promises! Forget about your father and his hatred for both of us!"

Madison blinked back her tears. The kettle whistled. Carmen set it on a cold burner and stood there with her back to Madison. She took a tissue out of her sweater pocket and dabbed her eyes and nose. "Just go, Madison. And take your money with you."

Madison lay her coat over her arm and picked up her purse. She eyed the envelope for a moment, wondering if she should take it with her. She left it where it was and headed for the door.

"If I take your damned money, will you leave my Ana alone?"

Madison turned back around, her hand on the doorknob. "I never intended to see her. She's the one—"

"That's a lie," Carmen said, interrupting her. "If Ana hadn't gone to the cemetery, you would have found a way. I see it in your eyes."

Madison dropped her gaze to the floor. Ana's mother was right. Madison would have run to Ana as fast as she could. The way she'd dreamed about so many times after her father's diagnosis.

"You didn't answer my question," Carmen said. "If I take your money, will you leave my daughter alone?"

"Yes, I will. It'll kill me, but I'll do it if you answer one question."

Carmen looked confused but nodded.

"Does Ana know who her father is?"

Carmen swayed where she stood. When she grabbed for the counter, Madison dropped her coat and purse and caught her right before she hit the floor.

2008

Madison was running late. She was due to meet Ana at a hotel in New Rochelle in thirty minutes. It wasn't an ideal scenario, but it was halfway between their schools and an easy train ride for Ana. One more month and she and Ana wouldn't have to meet in hotels anymore. She would graduate from Yale, and they would move in together for Ana's last year at Princeton. Of course, there was that pesky little issue of telling her father about their big plans. She'd put it off for as long as she could, but that conversation would have to happen soon.

Shit. The light was on in her father's library. She never should've gone home to pick up more clothes before meeting Ana. It had put her way behind. She rushed past the door, but her father's loud voice boomed into the hallway. "Madison!"

Madison dropped her weekender bag at the door and walked in. George was sitting behind his desk, smoking a cigar. "Sorry, Dad. I'm running late for a date." She kissed him on the cheek and went to leave again.

George cleared his throat, forcing her to stop and turn around. "A date? With who?"

"Just a guy from school," Madison lied. "You don't know him."

"That's because he doesn't exist." George snuffed out his cigar and leaned back in his chair. "You think I didn't see this coming? You think I don't have a contingency plan in place? How many times do I have to tell you, Madison? I won't sit back and watch you throw your life away for that girl! You're a Prescott. You have a duty to your family. Whatever this sick predilection is, you will control it!"

Madison knew better than to let out the huge sigh she was holding in. Predilection? Her father was so clueless. "Please, don't do this, Dad. Just let me live my life."

"Oh!" George casually waved his hand in the air. "Just let you live your life, huh? Just like that? Just pretend you don't have a legacy to protect?" He slammed his fist down on the desk. "Madison Prescott, I did not build this company into what it is today just to give it to a board of directors, or God forbid, my idiot sister. It's your duty to work for the family business. It's your duty to get married and have Prescott children. A *son*, preferably. You don't get to live this grand life and then just walk away from it because you feel like it. That's not how it works."

Madison's shoulders slumped. She walked back over to her father and got on her knees. "I will, Dad. I'll do everything you ask of me, but I can't marry a man. I just can't. I love Ana." She tapped her chest with her fist. "She is my heart. I've loved her since I was eight years old. Give me Ana, and I'll give you an heir. As many as you want. You can even pick the sperm donor. Just…please…don't deny me Ana."

"Oh, Christ, Madison. Don't cry. It's unbecoming." He shook his head. "And get up off the floor. Sit in a chair like a decent human being."

Madison wiped her tears away and moved to sit across the desk from her father. Losing Ana wasn't an option. She had a plan in place too. She'd set money aside. They'd get by until she found a job. Her grades were good. She had connections. It would be fine. Better than fine because she'd be free of George.

"What you're asking is inconceivable. You asking me to let my homosexual daughter—"

"No one uses that word anymore, Dad. People are gay. Lots of people are gay now."

"Silence!" George's face turned red. "You're asking me to let my homosexual daughter run my company and live in my ancestral home and raise my grandchildren with a…a…"

"A what, Dad? Say it. Say what you think Ana is. Because what she is, is a beautiful, intelligent, funny woman with a heart of gold. She's smarter than both of us combined. I have to work my ass off to get good grades, and Ana, she tutors people like me. Do you understand that? Do you understand that nothing will ever keep me from being with her?"

"You've been defying me for years on this subject. I've been far too lenient. It's time to put an end to it."

"This subject?" Madison stood up. "This is my life, Dad. Ana is my life. And if you can't accept that, I have nothing more to say to you." She walked out of the library, picked up her bag and was almost out of the house when her father's right-hand man grabbed her arm. She tried to yank her arm loose. "Let go of me, Albert."

"I can't. I have my orders, and they don't come from you." Albert grabbed Madison around the waist and picked her up just enough so he could carry her back to George's office, kicking and screaming.

"You fucking moron! You can't manhandle me like that!" Madison watched in shock as Albert locked the door behind him. She turned to her father. "Dad! Are you really going to let him do this to me? He just assaulted me!"

George waved Albert into the room. "Sit, Albert. We need to talk some sense into her." He pulled a folder out of his drawer and set it on his desk. "As we've discussed previously, Madison, you will start working at the company immediately. Then, you'll bring home someone of the male persuasion, and he'll ask me for your hand in marriage. Oh, and of course, you will never see or communicate with Ana Perez again. Not ever. If you do this, here's what Albert and I *won't* do." George tapped the folder with his finger a few times. He paused and took a deep breath. "Before I do this, I want you to know that you're very special to me, Madison. It pains me to take it this far, but you've given me no choice."

It wasn't that George never showed her any love. It was that his love came from the fact that she looked just like him. Same blue eyes. Same crooked smile that created a little dimple on her right cheek. He didn't care about what made her unique. He only cared about what made her his. "This is how you show me you care, Dad? By taking away the only good thing in my life?"

He turned to Albert and scoffed. "Did you hear that Albert? This girl is the only good thing in her life."

"I heard it, sir."

George stared at the folder on his desk before turning his attention back to Madison. "I've had just about enough of your petulant whining. Something tells me the maid's daughter has her eye on plenty of other good things in your life." George pushed the folder across the desk. "Albert, please explain to my daughter what we *won't* do once she lives up to what's expected of her."

Albert opened the folder and cleared his throat. "Number one. We won't plant drugs in Ana's apartment, effectively getting her arrested and kicked out of Princeton."

Madison's mouth gaped open. "You wouldn't!"

George remained stoic. "Continue, Albert."

"Number two. We won't bring it to Immigration's attention that Carmen Perez entered this country illegally and lives under a false name."

Madison shook her head in utter shock. "Since when do you care if your employees are here legally?"

"Shall I continue, sir?" George nodded, so Albert ceremoniously cleared his throat again. "Number three. We won't impede Ana Perez's efforts to get a job, buy a home, get a car loan, etcetera. In other words, we'll leave her good name and credit alone. Number four."

George put up his hand to stop Albert. "Are you getting the picture?"

Madison shook her head as tears filled her eyes. "I'll never forgive you for this. If you hurt her, you'll never see me again. I will *never* speak to you again!"

"You haven't even heard the worst of it." George waved a hand. "Go ahead, Albert."

"Number four. We won't let it be known to anyone that Carmen's real name is Margareta Fuentes, and Ana Perez is actually Ana Villareal, the daughter of Vincent Villareal—a very dangerous man who would not take kindly to having his unborn daughter stolen from him."

"They call him *El Serpiente*. The Snake," George said.

Madison's face paled. She needed to sit down before she collapsed.

"If you love her like you say you do, you'll let her find her own life," Albert said.

Madison turned to him. His voice was gentler than normal. That scared her even more because she knew that to some extent, this scared Albert too. "I want proof," she said, barely able to get the words out, her heart felt so broken. Albert handed her the file. She opened it and found newspaper clippings and mug shots. Vincent Villareal was indeed a real person.

Albert put his hand on her arm. "Imagine what would happen if *El Serpiente* found out he had a daughter in the states? Do you really think he'd let Carmen live very long? And what kind of future would Ana have? She has no family other than Carmen. And with her smarts and education, her father would undoubtedly use her for his own purposes. She'd be forced to join his corrupt world. She'd be recruited."

Madison looked at him with questioning eyes. "What?"

"He's a powerful man, Madison. He's connected. Mafia. Drug cartels. Imagine how helpful she'd be to him with her degree in finance."

"Stop." Madison closed the folder. The blood had returned to her cheeks. She eyed both of them for a moment. "I'll never forgive either of you for this. Ever. And Albert, you better hope my father lives to a ripe old age because he's the only one who can protect you. You're taking my life from me and don't think I'll hesitate for one second to take yours from you."

George chuckled. "Welcome to the real world, Madison. Now, let's get to work, shall we? You'll need a business wardrobe. I'll hire a stylist to help with that. Your hair should be shorter. More professional."

Madison tuned out. All she could think about was Ana waiting for her at the hotel. She'd be worried by now. She excused herself and went to the restroom, claiming she felt nauseated. She barely got the door locked before she fell to her knees and grabbed the toilet. After emptying the contents of her stomach, she leaned against the wall and pulled out her phone. There were already five messages from Ana.

How could she do it? How could she write the words? And what would those words even be? She started typing, but she couldn't see a thing through the tears. She waited a minute and wiped her eyes dry. It would have to be quick. No conversation. One final text message would have to do.

Can't make it. I'm so sorry. Don't call.

No words would be right. There was no right way to say it. Those would have to do. She pushed herself up the wall. Albert was just outside the door. She could hear him pacing. She opened the door and he held out his hand. "Your phone, Madison. We'll get you a new one for work."

Madison handed it over. "You'll pay for this one day." Her father stood a few feet away. She glared at him before heading for the stairs. Madison felt herself change in that moment. She'd always had a contentious relationship with her father, but now he was the enemy. If she ever smiled, it wouldn't be for him. If she laughed, she'd make sure he didn't hear it. And she promised herself that one day, she'd bury her father with her own hands.

Present Day

Carmen took the offered tissue from Madison. She wiped her brow and then dabbed her nose. She'd almost fainted when Madison had mentioned Ana's father. There wasn't any question in her mind that Madison knew exactly who he was. Otherwise, there would be no reason to bring him up.

"I was young and in love once," Carmen said. "My story isn't so different from yours and Ana's. Except for the pregnancy. And the violence." She shrugged. "Maybe it's not the same at all, now that I think about it."

"He was a powerful man. You made the right decision," Madison said.

"Vincent wasn't a powerful man. He was just a kid like me." Carmen set her stare on Madison. "It was his family that I had to fear. Had they found out about me—a girl who came from nothing—they would've taken my baby and raised Ana as their own."

"So, you ran."

Carmen focused on Ana's picture hanging on the wall. "I didn't know who Vincent was when I met him. I didn't know he was the son of one of the most corrupt politicians in Mexico. He was just a sweet boy, and I thought he loved me, so I let him make love to me, and not long after that, I could feel the little life growing inside of me."

"Did you tell him you were pregnant?"

"He never wanted me to meet his family. He always had an excuse. So, one night, I followed him home, and I got the shock of my life when I saw where he lived behind that big security gate. At first, I thought this was a good thing. My baby would grow up in a nice environment and get a good education. But then, I got a horrible feeling in my heart. And something told me that I had to find out exactly who Vincent was before I told him about our child." Carmen shook her head in despair. "I asked around, and everyone got a look of fear in their eyes when I mentioned Vincent's family."

"So, his father is the bad man, not Vincent?"

Carmen waved a finger. "Don't be fooled by my description of the boy I once knew. Vincent is far worse than his father ever was."

"How did you get away?"

Carmen's eyes misted over. "I lied to everyone I loved. I told Vincent I was going to Vera Cruz to visit an aunt. I told my parents I was going to the city to visit a friend. I told everyone I could think of a different story, and then I ran for the border. I found a distant relative in Texas who took me in until Ana was born. Then, I changed my name and never looked back. Not until today."

Madison slid closer on the sofa and took Carmen into her arms. "You did the right thing."

Carmen crumpled into Madison's arms, her pain coming out in deep sobs. "I gave up everything for my child. And every day, I pray for my parents' forgiveness. I pray that they would do the same thing if they had to."

"They would." Madison held Carmen until she calmed down. Then she took her hands and looked her in the eye. "Ana doesn't ever need to know about her father. This secret will die with me. I promise you that."

Carmen had almost forgotten what it felt like to fear for her life. She was nineteen years old when she'd crossed the border with only the clothes on her back. Now, at fifty-five, she was really only worried about one person. "Can you keep her safe, Madison? I don't care about me anymore. I've lived my life, but my Ana…" She squeezed Madison's hand. "*Our* Ana…she still has so much life left to live."

"I promise you, on my bastard of a father's grave, that Ana will never have to worry about this. She will never know who her real father is, even if that means she hates me for the rest of her life."

Carmen studied Madison's eyes. It was a face she knew so well. "You're still who you used to be. It's hard to believe after everything that happened, but you still love her?"

Madison bit her lip as tears filled her eyes. She didn't say the words, but a slight nod told Carmen it was true.

"My God," Carmen whispered. "Tell me what happened. Why did you ask Ana to marry you and then walk away?"

Madison shook her head.

"Was it this? Did you find out about Vincent and get scared for your family? I would understand—"

Madison shook her head again. "No. I would never have made that choice. It was made for me. You and I aren't so different after all. We both had to give up everything."

"Your father." Carmen took a deep breath. "This is why you buried him the way you did?"

"Somewhere along the way, you made a mistake," Madison said. "You left a trail to your past, and my father found it. He knew who you were, and he threatened to ruin Ana's life and reveal who you both really were to Vincent and his family. I couldn't let that happen."

"And all you had to do in return was stay away from Ana?"

Madison chuckled. "And marry a wealthy white man and work in the family business and give George an heir. Little things," she joked.

Carmen looked at Ana's picture again. "You could've defied your father. You could've run away with my Ana. Disappeared. Taken her from me. But you didn't."

Madison's smile faded. "It wasn't honorable, what I did. It was just…the only option."

Carmen teared up again. "I'm so sorry my past ruined your future."

"You didn't ruin it; my father did. Please, don't ever feel guilty for wanting to give your child a better life. I mean, just look at her! She's an amazing woman, and you, Mrs. Perez, can take full credit for that."

"Would you please call me Carmen? After all we've been through? And besides, now you know I'm not really a 'Mrs.'" Carmen tried to smile, but it was unconvincing.

"Yes. I'd like that," Madison said. "And I want you to know that your daughter is the most incredible person I've ever known."

Carmen felt proud of what she'd accomplished, raising a child on her own. But she also knew there were others who helped shape the woman Ana had become. "I have to think you had something to do with that too," she said, taking Madison's hand into her own. "She was such a happy child. A happy teenager. So very happy until that day."

"So was I, once you two showed up." Madison smiled. "Do you know how important you both were to me, Carmen? You were like a mother to me."

Carmen placed a gentle kiss on Madison's cheek. "You were a precious child. I loved you dearly."

Madison wrapped her arms around Carmen and held on to her. "Thank you for saying that," she whispered. "I've missed you both so much. Not a day has gone by—" She pulled back so they were eye to eye. "Tell me about her. Everything. Please. I've missed so much of her life."

Carmen offered her another tissue and took one for herself. "She makes me so proud to be her mother, but she works too hard. She tells me that a woman on Wall Street has to work twice as hard as a man, but I think she works *three* times as hard as them."

Madison nodded. "And does she ever have fun?"

"She rides almost every weekend. It's the one thing she makes sure she has time for."

"Rides?"

"Horses," Carmen said. "She always wanted to ride like you did. She gave herself her first horse for her twenty-seventh birthday."

"Oh God." Madison blinked back the tears.

"It's okay." Carmen patted Madison's leg. "Ana knew it was your father's rules that kept her from the stables, not yours. She never begrudged you that."

Madison grabbed another tissue and wiped her eyes. "I wanted to give Ana everything. The world." She put her hand on Carmen's again. "Tell me more."

Carmen thought about it for a moment. "My Ana is gay. Not bisexual. Just gay. She has made that very clear to me. And she's only ever dated women." She kept her eyes set on Madison. She wanted to see her reaction to that pronouncement. "I used to blame that on you, but I eventually came to realize that it's just who Ana is. She's a strong, powerful woman who is attracted to strong, powerful women."

Madison pursed her lips together. She dropped her face in her hands and gasped for breath, her emotions bubbling to the surface. "I wanted to be her wife," she whispered. "Ana should've been my wife."

Carmen placed her hand on Madison's shoulder, letting her cry for a moment before she replied. "I know that now, Madison. And maybe Ana should know that too."

"No." Madison grabbed another tissue. "We can't tell her that without telling her the whole truth. And that's something we can't risk. My father may be dead, but hers isn't."

Carmen wrung her hands. It was almost too much to bear. The past was catching up to all of them. But she could see it in Madison's eyes and hear it in her voice, the love she still had for Ana. And a question popped into her head—one she'd never been brave enough to ask her own daughter. "If you don't mind my asking, how do two little girls decide they're—" Carmen shook her head. "Never mind. It's not my place."

Madison got up and picked her purse up off the floor where she'd dropped it when Carmen had collapsed. She sat back down and opened her wallet. Tucked behind her cash was an old photo of Ana and Madison. She held it out. "Do you remember taking this photo of us?"

Carmen took the photo. "Yes. Did Ana give this to you?"

"When I left for Yale. Look on the back."

Carmen turned it over. "Madison G. Prescott and Ana M.M. Perez equals forever." She turned it back over and ran her finger over the two young girls. "My little angels."

"She gave me two copies in case I lost one. I still have both."

Carmen smiled. "You two would have made quite the power couple, as they say."

"She was my whole world," Madison said. "So different from all of the stuck-up kids I went to school with. And so much smarter than any of them. We were the best of friends. And then, something changed. The way she looked at me changed. The way I looked back at her changed." Madison chuckled. "Maybe I shouldn't be saying these things to you, Carmen."

Carmen grinned. "Well, I'm the one who asked. Please, tell me. I've always wondered."

"The first time we kissed was on her seventeenth birthday, and I never wanted to kiss anyone else after that. I knew in that moment that Ana was who I wanted to spend my life with."

"And your father used me to deprive you of that."

"He did. Very successfully. I did exactly what he wanted me to do so Ana could live her life. Because if there's one thing I knew about my dad, it's that he rarely made idle threats. He always followed through. And I couldn't risk him hurting Ana."

Carmen looked her in the eye. "Did you love the man you married?"

Madison took a deep breath. "In so many ways, my wedding day was the worst day of my life. But it did the trick. George didn't interfere in Ana's life the way he'd threatened to."

Carmen slumped forward and made the sign of the cross. Through her tears, she said, "I need to ask God for forgiveness."

"For what?"

"I wished for terrible things. I wished for your divorce. I wished many bad things for you."

"It's okay, Carmen. I wouldn't blame you if you'd wished me dead."

Carmen looked up at her. "I did."

Madison smiled and put her arm around Carmen. "And now? Do you still wish me dead?"

Carmen shook her head. "No. I wish you were my daughter-in-law."

Madison kissed Carmen's cheek. "Me too."

CHAPTER EIGHT

A na glanced at her watch as she rode the elevator up to the twenty-eighth floor. Why didn't her mother understand that this was completely unnecessary? So what if her mom hadn't fully realized what she'd been given? And yeah, it was nice of Madison to show up at her mother's apartment, but this? Why did Ana have to go and personally thank her? It was her mom who was the sudden millionaire, not Ana. But she'd insisted on a proper thank you on behalf of both of them. Her mom had always been one for manners, but this was just weird. Ana suddenly worried that her mom might be suffering the early stages of senility. In her mid-fifties. Maybe this was a latent punishment for that lamp she broke when she was eleven. Or maybe her mom had simply decided, quite suddenly, to hate her. All were completely plausible explanations, and Ana would have come up with more had the elevator ride not been inexplicably fast.

Showing up unannounced at lunchtime would most assuredly mean Ana could tell her mother she'd tried but just had no luck because Madison was a very busy woman. She could drop off the homemade cookies her mother had made and be done with it. No need to return the Tupperware. Her mom had plenty, thank you very much.

The redhead standing next to her was eyeing the cookies. Ana shrugged. "My mom. She thinks cookies make everything better."

The woman smiled. "I would have to agree with your mother."

Ana opened the lid. "Have one. They're chocolate chunk. Heavy on the chunk."

"Thank you." The woman took a cookie. "And thank your mother for me."

They stepped off of the elevator together, headed in the same direction. Ana stopped short at the big glass door. Was she really going to enter Madison's world again? Willingly? Was she *insane*? Yes, she had most definitely lost her damned mind.

The woman opened the door. "Are you coming in?"

"Yes." Ana forced a smile. "Thank you." She walked up to the receptionist's desk, cookies in hand. "Ana Perez to see Madison Fairmont." She knew Madison didn't use her married name, but she wanted to say it anyway. Out loud. To remind herself. Ha! As if she needed a reminder.

"Ms. Prescott is in a meeting. May I give her a message?"

Ana put up her hand. "That's fine. I'll catch her another time."

The nice redhead from the elevator stepped forward. "I can take care of this, Susan." She turned to Ana. "I'm Jocelyn, Madison's assistant. I think she's—" Jocelyn looked over Ana's shoulder. "Right here, actually."

Ana turned to look. Madison stood at the conference room door, chatting with someone as the rest of the group filed out of the room. *Shit.* Ana stood there, motionless, wondering if she should drop the cookies and run. But it was too late. Their eyes met, and Madison froze too.

Drop the cookies and run! Ana flinched. Jocelyn's warm hand on her shoulder was unexpected. "I met your mother the other day. Mrs. Perez?"

Ana wondered how many shades of red she was turning. "Yes." She cleared her throat, hoping to sound more convincing. "Yes, that's my mother. If Madison is busy—"

"I'm not. Clear my schedule, Joss." Madison stood a few feet away.

Ana wanted to grab Jocelyn's arm and beg her not to leave her standing there all alone with Madison, but it was too late. Jocelyn was out of reach and walking toward what Ana could only assume was Madison's office.

"Hi," Madison said. Her voice was softer than it had been a second ago when she gave Joss an order. Ana knew that voice. And hearing it made her breath catch in her throat. For a moment, she'd forgotten why she was even there. *Madison.* The name kept repeating in her head. All the times she'd whispered it, yelled it, written it in love letters. All the times that name had been preceded with a "Why?" *Why, Maddy? Why did you stop loving me?* And then, she remembered why she was there. And her jaw flexed.

Madison took a step closer, the concerned wrinkle in her brow deepening. "Ana?"

Don't come any closer! Ana wanted to scream those words. She wanted to scream a lot of words, none of which were appropriate for the current setting. She couldn't yell, *Don't look at me like you care, Maddy! Because you don't fucking care! You never did!* Saying it in her head would have to do. "Do you have a minute?" Yes, those were the appropriate words.

"Of course. This way."

"That's not necessary." Ana had no desire to be alone with Madison in her office. She didn't trust herself to be civil. All her mother asked was that she deliver the cookies and offer a word of thanks. That could easily be accomplished right where they were. She held out the cookies. "These aren't from me. I don't really, you know, cook. Or I guess, bake, in this case. They're from my mom. She made them for you. It's a new recipe, not like the ones she used to make for us when we were young with the cheap chocolate chips. I mean, those were good too. We loved those. But these have chunks of the good stuff. And also, your favorite—coconut." Ana noticed that the receptionist was staring at them with wide, very interested eyes. She also noticed that Madison's look of concern had morphed into a big, happy grin.

"Please. My office." Madison took the cookies and started walking.

Ana glanced at the receptionist again. She was still staring and probably feeling rather amused by Ana's little cookie speech, with the stumbling over every other word thing. Ana sighed and hurried to catch up to Madison.

She tried not to look at the pictures on the walls. She had no desire to see the life Madison had lived without her. She was good enough for a childhood lived in the secret hiding places of their youth. She was even good enough for the teenage and college years, also lived mostly in secret. Good enough to be Madison's first love, her first lover, even. But when it came time to live in this world, the real world, the world of fortunes and futures and families, Ana had definitely not been good enough. The proof was hanging all over the walls.

"You still wear it," Madison said from behind her.

Ana lifted an eyebrow. "What?"

"*J'Adore*. You still wear it."

Oh God. Why hadn't she thought of that when she was getting dressed? She'd thought of everything else. The ivory skirt was the tightest one she owned. The black satin heels were not her usual work attire. And the black silk blouse clung to her curves more than the others in her closet. On the off chance that she'd see Madison today, she wanted to look her best. To let Madison know what she'd been missing all these years, Ana had pored over every detail. Except the perfume. Habits.

Yes, Ana still wore it. Always had. But she didn't want to talk about her perfume, and she certainly didn't want to have to look Madison in the eye, so she turned to a different wall, and right there in front of her was a photo of Scott Fairmont. She hated that Madison's husband was so goddamned handsome. Every straight girl's dream, she imagined. His hand was on Madison's hip, exactly where Ana used to put her hand when they would walk arm in arm.

When they were young, they'd walk all over the estate arm in arm. Madison was taller, so she would drape her arm over Ana's shoulder, always avoiding her braids because Ana had a tender head and hated having her hair pulled.

Ana's hand was always on Madison's waist. That is, until they became more than friends. Her hand naturally landed a little lower after that, on Madison's hip. Right where Scott Fairmont's hand was in that damned photograph.

"I'm engaged," Ana blurted out. She squeezed her eyes shut. God, she was making a fool of herself. She wasn't really engaged. Not even close. God, why did she say that?

There was a long pause before Madison said, "I'm happy for you. Carmen spoke very highly of her."

Ana turned so they were face-to-face. "My mom told you about her?" She wondered what other information her mother had divulged. Had her mother told Madison that her daughter was so obsessed with making a name for herself that she'd forgotten to really live? When was the last time she'd dipped her foot in a pool or watched a sunset? Ana couldn't honestly recall. Damn her mother for putting her in this position.

Madison took a step back and leaned on the front of her desk, gripping the edge with both hands. "A doctor. Your mother approves."

Madison's voice sounded a bit shaky to Ana, and it seemed as if she'd leaned on her desk for support, but Ana was probably just imagining that. "Yes. Kris is her name."

Madison's smile seemed genuine, but Ana couldn't hold her stare for long. She was drawn to those long legs. Her eyes fluttered closed as she tried to block out the memories of what it felt like to have them wrapped around her. When she opened them again and spotted the scar on Madison's knee, one specific memory came flooding back as if it'd happened yesterday.

2006

"Ooh, that's gonna leave a scar." Ana inspected the wound closely. "Did you go to the nurse and get some antiseptic cream? You know the dorm showers are a hotbed of bacteria. You really should have gotten stitches." She sighed. "It's too late now, I suppose."

Madison lifted her knee so Ana could tuck a pillow under it. "That's exactly what the nurse said, my little germaphobe. Now, where's my kiss hello?"

Ana covered the wound back up with the bandage and took off her jean jacket. "Sorry. I had to make sure you'd live first." She leaned down and kissed her softly. "How did it happen?"

"A stupid fall on the tennis court. I was trying to beat my friend, Scott. I've told you about him, right?" Madison reached up and pulled the necklace out from beneath Ana's shirt. "Put it on."

"You have too many friends to count at Yale. I can't keep track of them all." Ana took the engagement ring off the chain and slipped it onto her ring finger. She held her hand out and wiggled her fingers. "Is this where you like it?"

Madison took her hand and kissed it. "Yeah. That's better. And I really don't have that many friends. Not friends I trust anyway. But I trust Scott, and I told him all about us."

Ana sat on the edge of the bed. "You told someone about us? Maddy, what if it gets back to your dad before you have a chance to tell him yourself?"

"I told you, I trust Scott. He hates how my father is constantly interfering in my life. His parents are the same way." Madison sat up and held Ana's face in her hand. She caressed her cheek with her thumb. "Don't worry. I know what I'm doing."

Ana gave her an unconvincing nod. "Okay."

"I have a room reserved at the hotel." Madison ran her thumb across Ana's bottom lip. "Please, tell me you can stay overnight."

"I have a ton of homework, and I have to be back at Princeton by noon for a tutoring session."

"Plenty of time." Madison leaned in for a kiss. "I want you tonight."

Ana put her hands on Madison's shoulders and pushed her back so they were eye to eye. "Can you even walk?"

Madison shrugged. "I can walk. I just can't…kneel on it."

"Ooh. You can't kneel on it. Hmm, I guess this means you'll be on your back tonight." Ana wagged her eyebrows. "All mine to do whatever I want with."

Madison grinned. "I'm always all yours to do whatever you want with, but what did you have in mind?"

Ana leaned in and nuzzled Madison's ear. "Naughty things. Things we've talked about but never did before."

"You mean…"

Ana turned and checked to make sure the door to the tiny room was shut. She took Madison's hand in hers and said, "I'm ready for more. I want to do everything with you. I want to be yours in every way, Maddy. And I want you to be mine." She squeezed Madison's hand and took a deep breath. "I've been thinking about it a lot, and I really want you in my mouth. All of you."

Madison grinned. "Let's go then."

Present Day

"She's a doctor," Ana said. "My doctor. Well, not anymore, but I had a heart thing." She felt as if she'd forgotten how to use the English language. *A heart thing?*

"Oh my God." Madison looked concerned. "Are you okay?"

Ana turned away again. Looking at Madison made her want to cry and yell and throw things. "Turned out it was just stress. And I should go."

"Ana."

Ana stopped but didn't turn around. "It's too hard, Maddy. I don't want to say something I'll regret."

"Isn't that all we have? Regrets? Just say it."

Ana turned back around. "I just came to say thank you for thinking of my mom and the others. She's so—" Ana didn't want to say the word *happy*. It would sound as if all these years neither of them had found any happiness. That wasn't true. Her mom had cried tears of happiness every time Ana had reached another impossible milestone in her career. "She's happy you remembered her. She's grateful. Very grateful. Hence, the cookies and this very awkward moment. She asked me to come here today."

"That's what you're supposed to say, but what do you really want to say?"

Ana glanced at the photograph of Scott again. In her mind, she replaced him with herself: Maddy and Ana, at whatever event it was that had them in formal dress. "I just wondered if straight girls ever regret their youthful indiscretions." There. She'd said it. And whatever happened next didn't really matter because what did she have to lose?

Madison's shoulders drooped as she let out a big sigh. "I wouldn't know."

Ana shook her head and chuckled. "You completely forgot about me, didn't you? No regrets, no memories. Just poof and I was gone." She scanned the other photographs. Her eyes landed on the one with President Obama. "I get it, Maddy. If you'd married me, that picture wouldn't even exist. Someone like you doesn't take the maid's daughter to the White House."

Madison pushed off the desk and stood right in front of Ana. "You couldn't be more wrong."

They were eye to eye, Ana's heels making her match Madison in height. She needed some sort of emotional knife. She wanted to stab at Madison's heart. Make her feel some pain. Something. Anything that would let her walk out of that office with her head held high. And then it came to her. Loyalty. Maddy was the most loyal person Ana had ever known until the day she broke her heart. And so, she wondered—had Madison been a faithful wife? And with one word, could Ana destroy the sanctity of that marriage? She reached out and touched Madison's cheek. "Beautiful," she whispered.

Madison's eyes shuttered closed as she leaned into the touch. She blinked them open again, and Ana saw tears. She hadn't expected tears. She took a step closer and cupped both cheeks. What was she doing? This was not what she'd intended. "Maddy," she whispered, not knowing what words would follow.

Madison took Ana's wrist and kissed the palm of her hand. "Ana." Madison's other hand slid around her waist. She pulled Ana to her, forcing them into a hug. "God, I've missed you."

There was nowhere for Ana's arms to go except around Madison's shoulders. She rested her hand on the back of Madison's head when she felt her start to shake. Madison was crying in her arms and holding her so tight around the waist, there was no escaping. Ana wasn't even sure she wanted to.

It felt the same, minus the tears. Maddy holding her as if she would never let her go felt exactly like it had fifteen years ago, warm and sensual and perfect. Were there words for this moment? If there were, Ana couldn't find them. All she could do was hold on.

For a moment, Ana let herself pretend. She heard the comforting words in her head that she would have for Madison in her moments of distress. Bad day at work, an argument with her father—the reason for the tears didn't matter. All that mattered was that Ana was there, trying to make it better with strong arms and soft words. *It's okay, baby. It'll be okay. I've got you.*

A knock on the door made Maddy pull away, and reality came crashing down around Ana again in the form of a handsome man standing there, looking at them. Madison was staring out the window now, with her back to both of them. And Ana's eyes met Scott's for the first time.

So, this was Scott Fairmont—the man who had stolen her fiancée. The person who was good enough, in George Prescott's eyes, to marry his daughter. Good God, he was even more handsome in real life. Ana averted her eyes. She was glad she hadn't said the words out loud. Because it would never be okay. Madison had made her choice. And that choice wasn't Ana.

"Sorry, I didn't realize you had company," Scott said.

Ana glanced at Madison, but she was still turned away. Time seemed to stop, leaving them in an eternally awkward moment. She was torn between leaving and walking over to Madison. She didn't know what she would say. Anger and love were fighting an unwinnable battle in her head. She still hadn't moved from the spot where they'd held each other a moment ago. "I was just leaving," she said, hoping Madison would turn around.

Scott offered his hand. "I'm Scott Fairmont. You must be Ana."

Surprised that he knew who she was, Ana took his hand. "Ana Perez." She glanced at Madison again, but she hadn't moved from the window. "I, um…" *Turn around, Maddy.* She desperately wanted to escape the horror of the situation, but she refused to do it until Madison turned around and looked at her one last time. She pushed her short hair behind her ears and waited a few more seconds. Finally, she said, "I was just inviting you and Maddy…Madison…to my engagement party." Yes. Because she wasn't already deep enough in the lie. She cringed at herself but managed a smile for Scott.

"Oh! Who's the lucky…" Scott stopped and glanced at Madison

Madison finally turned around. She leaned against the windowsill and wiped her nose with a tissue. "Who's the lucky woman? Her name is Kris. And we'd love to come."

Ana breathed a sigh of relief. She wasn't relieved that Madison had accepted an invitation to a party that might not even happen, just that she'd finally turned around. She needed to see those blue eyes one more time before she left. Their connection had been broken so abruptly it almost felt as if Madison was being yanked out of her arms and her heart. Again. "We haven't set a date yet, but I'll let you know."

Madison gave her a barely perceptible nod, then ducked her head. The silence felt deafening, and seconds felt like hours, but Ana found herself not wanting to leave. Madison was in pain, and she couldn't bear seeing that.

Taking away Madison's pain had always been Ana's job, but it belonged to another now. She finally pulled her eyes away from Madison and focused on Scott. "Good to meet you, Scott."

"Good to meet you too, Ana. I've heard so much—" Scott glanced at Madison. "Anyway, we look forward to meeting your fiancée."

Ana had to look one more time. Her eyes met Madison's again and stayed there for another awkward moment. "Bye, Maddy," she whispered.

"Thank your mother for me." Madison bit her quivering lip. "For the cookies." She turned back to the window, leaving Ana and Scott to look at only one another again.

Ana went to the door, and Scott opened it for her. She took one more look at Madison and then left.

CHAPTER NINE

I'm so sorry I barged in like that. Are you okay?" Scott closed the door behind Ana.

Was Madison okay? No. And she never would be. "I can't tell her the truth. All I can do is tell more lies."

"Your father is dead, Maddy. He can't come back from the grave. Maybe it's time."

Madison wasn't so sure. She'd been having nightmares about George doing just that. Clawing his way out of the dirt while she and Ana desperately tried to bury him. She'd woken up in a sweat more than once. "I promised Carmen. We both agree that it would kill Ana if she knew the truth."

"And you're never going to tell me what that truth is, are you?"

Madison turned to face him. There was no one in the world she trusted more than Scott. "Sit down."

❖

Scott leaned forward, resting his elbows on his knees. "Jesus," he said as he loosened his tie. He thought back to all the times George had professed his love for his daughter. "She's just like me," he would say. "Spittin' image of the old man." But Scott knew better. Madison was nothing like her old man. "This isn't your burden to bear, Maddy. It's Carmen's. She should do the right thing and tell Ana. She owes you that."

Madison stopped pacing. "To what end? So Ana can live in fear and shame for the rest of her life? She doesn't deserve that. And if it weren't for my father and that bastard, Albert…"

Scott's eyes widened. "Albert."

"What about him?"

"The second your dad died, you kicked him out on the street! Literally!"

"I wanted him to know what it felt like! I wanted him to experience the humiliation of having your belongings thrown into the street! I wanted—" Madison grabbed her forehead. "Oh God."

Scott stood. "He knows everything about Ana's father. He could use that against both of you. He could put Ana in danger."

Madison went to her desk and hit the intercom button. "Joss! Find Albert! Now!" She turned back to Scott. "Find him. Oh my God, find him!"

Scott grabbed his suit jacket. "I'm on it."

Jocelyn bolted out of her chair as Scott ran past her. "Mr. Fairmont!" she called after Scott, "What the hell is going on?"

Scott went back to Jocelyn's desk. "We have to find Albert. If you know where he hangs out, what bars he goes to, anything."

Jocelyn picked up the phone. "I'll see what I can find out."

Kris poured syrup on her waffle. "You saw her again? I don't know how I feel about that. I mean, I know you needed to go to the funeral to find closure."

Ana took a sip of the hospital coffee and grimaced. "God, that's awful."

"The coffee here is fine. You're just a coffee snob."

"Then your taste buds are numb. And what do you mean you don't know how you feel about it? I had to thank her for making my mom a millionaire, didn't I?"

"Blood money." Kris took another big bite of the waffle and stared at Ana as she chewed.

"Don't look at me like that. It's not blood money. Ten people got the same deal. All of them were former or current long-term employees of the bastard. Maddy didn't owe them anything."

"Maddy? She's Maddy now?"

"She was always Maddy," Ana said.

Kris dropped her fork. "You have never once called her Maddy. Madison, Mrs. Fairmont, Mrs. Trust fund, gay for a day, two-faced liar, thief, heartbreaker—"

Ana reached for Kris' hand. "And that last one, you fixed. Now, do you want to get married or not?"

Ana hadn't expected such hesitation when she'd brought up the subject of marriage a few minutes earlier. She figured Kris would jump for joy that they were even talking about it, which Ana had always refused to do in the past.

Kris narrowed her eyes. She took another bite and stared at Ana again as if she were trying to read her mind. "Why now? What's changed?"

Ana looked at her watch. She didn't have time for this. She needed to get back to work. "Nothing's changed."

"I asked you to marry me two years ago, Ana. You said you couldn't, and then we never talked about it again. So, why now? Why are you accepting the proposal right after seeing Madison again?"

"Because you're not Madison," Ana said. "And maybe it took her coming back into my life for me to realize that."

Kris shook her head. "I can't meet her. I can't be friends with her. You can't expect me to suddenly be okay with the person who broke you into so many little pieces it took me five years to put you back together again."

"Well, that sucks." Ana took another sip of Kris' coffee and grimaced again. "Nope. Still bad."

Kris pulled the cup to her side of the table. "Why does it suck? Do you really want Madison in your life after what she did?"

Ana shrugged. "It helped. Seeing her again somehow helped. I'm not sure why. I guess just confirmation that we're different people now, you know?" She looked at her watch again. Either Kris still wanted to marry her or she didn't. Why couldn't she just answer the damned question?

Kris's phone vibrated on the table. She stood and moved to Ana's side of the table. "I have to go. Can we talk about this later?" She leaned in for a kiss.

"It's not really up for discussion. I invited Madison to our engagement party."

Kris straightened back up. "Our what?"

Ana grabbed Kris's lab coat and pulled her down to eye level. "You've wanted this for two years, and now, I'm giving it to you. So, you should just kiss me. And eventually, marry me."

Kris leaned down again. "I do want to marry you. I just want to make sure that you're sure." She kissed Ana's forehead. "Gotta run."

Was Ana sure? She was sure that Kris could handle her. She was strong enough. Kris had proven herself over the years as a person Ana could count on. A person who could ride out the bad times, when Ana couldn't handle anyone getting too close to her. And Kris knew Ana's history. She understood what Ana had been through.

Their first six months of dating had been "Madison-free." Ana had successfully hidden her wounds like she'd done with every other woman she'd dated. That was until March third rolled around, the date that Madison had asked Ana to marry her. Kris had found Ana sobbing in her shower, and over the next few months, she'd managed to get the entire story out of her. A story that Ana hadn't ever told anyone before that.

Kris was a good person. She never made promises she couldn't keep. She never left texts or voice mails unanswered, and she always let Ana know when she would be late. Their relationship wasn't perfect. It wasn't exactly simmering with passion, but it was steady. Ana always knew what to expect. And Kris' long hours suited them both.

Ana could start by telling Kris that she loved her. Sure, she always said it at the door or on the phone when she said good-bye. A quick "love you" that wasn't much different from how she talked to her mom.

It was the "I love you" when looking Kris in the eye that was hard. The "I love you" after having sex that she never seemed to want to say. The words were there sometimes, in the back of her mind. Kris was right, after all, when she said she'd put Ana back together. So, why couldn't she ever say the words?

She'd never said them to anyone but Madison, that was why. And she'd promised herself that no one would ever have that much power over her emotions again.

That needed to change. Ana stood and ran after Kris. If they were going to get married, Kris deserved to hear the words. The big, metal doors were about to close, so Ana shouted, "Kris!"

The doors closed, but they opened again. Kris walked up to her. "What's wrong?"

"Nothing. I just—" Ana stepped closer. Her heart was beating hard in her chest. "I did that all wrong. It wasn't romantic; it wasn't what you deserve."

Kris chuckled. "Since when are you the romantic type? You hate romance. You spit in the face of romance."

Ana put her fingers on Kris's lips to quiet her. "Okay. I get it. I'm not good at that stuff, but I—" She stopped and took a breath. *Just tell her you love her!* "You're such a catch. I know I'd be lucky to have you."

"Me too." Kris leaned in and kissed her cheek. "I have to run. There's a broken ankle waiting for me."

"Okay." Ana forced a smile. "Yeah, okay. I'll see you later." She'd have to find the words. Before they got married, she'd have to find the words.

❖

It was rare that Madison ever asked to stop anywhere on the way home. She didn't really have to run errands. Not with all of the domestic staff and office help she had at her disposal. It was only for personal gifts that she ever shopped. Even her wardrobe was handled by a stylist who met with her at the office.

So, when Madison said she wanted to make a stop on the way home to buy flowers, Stephen was surprised. When she told him she wanted to stop at her father's grave after that, he was dumbfounded.

He found the nearest flower stand and watched with curiosity as Madison carefully chose stems of yellow and pink roses, creating her own bouquet. By the time they got to the cemetery, clouds had moved in. Stephen put the car in park and turned around. "Would you like the umbrella, ma'am?"

Madison opened her door before Stephen could get out of the car. "We'll be fine. Come with me, Stephen."

"Yes, ma'am."

They walked to the gravesite together, Stephen's hands tucked deep in his pockets. He felt nervous, not sure what he'd do if Madison got emotional again. He didn't know the right words to use. Saying everything would be all right seemed good, even if it was just speculation. Hopefully, they would just place the flowers on the grave and walk away without incident this time.

The sun broke through the clouds. Madison looked at the sky and smiled. Stephen's eyes were on her shoes. He didn't want her to break another heel walking in the uneven grass. "Ma'am," he said, offering his arm.

"Thank you, Stephen."

Sod covered the gravesite, and a temporary marker was firmly set in place. Stephen wondered if Madison had ordered the gravestone yet—what words she'd use to describe her father. You couldn't really put "asshole" on a gravestone, could you?

They stood in silence for a moment, and then Madison said, "He's still dead. I had to make sure."

"Yes, ma'am." Stephen shot her a glance and looked away. *Please, don't cry.*

Madison took a few steps to the left, bent down, and placed the flowers on her mother's grave. She took a tissue out of her purse and wiped the dust off of the granite.

Stephen took a closer look at the marker. There were no kind words for the woman. It didn't say beloved wife and mother like some he'd seen. It was basic. Way too basic for a Prescott. The corner of his mouth turned up because he knew Madison would give her father nothing more in the way of a grave marker than he'd given his own wife. Nothing fancy. Basic.

Madison pointed to a bench. "Sit with me."

Stephen nodded and followed her. She sat down and took a deep breath, staring at her father's gravesite through her dark sunglasses. "He was such a bastard, Stephen. He ruined my life."

Stephen clasped his hands together so they wouldn't shake. Conversations weren't easy for him at the best of times, and this kind of thing made his throat go dry. But he was pretty sure who Madison was talking about, and if he could help his boss, he most definitely would try. "Ms. Perez, ma'am?"

Madison huffed out a laugh. "Yeah. Ms. Perez."

Stephen swallowed hard. "You…loved her, ma'am?"

Madison smiled. "I adored her. She was my whole world, and he took her from me." She furrowed her brow and looked Stephen in the eye. "Don't ever tell your daughter who she can and can't love."

Stephen relaxed a little bit as he chuckled. "No, ma'am." He held up his little finger. "She has me right here."

"I remember when she was born. You were a mess of a father. A total wreck, thinking you'd never be able to do right by her. But look at her now, Stephen."

"Yes, ma'am."

There was a time when Stephen didn't believe he'd ever have a family. Who would want a broody, awkward guy like him? But Madison made him see things in himself he couldn't see. Things like how good he was with his hands. How he could fix just about anything, be it a car engine or a toaster. And he was loyal. She said women really liked a loyal man.

And then there were the physical traits like his full head of hair. His mom always called it unruly, but Madison had given him some pomade and taught him how to comb it.

She'd convinced him there was a girl out there who would like his quiet, gentle nature. He just had to find her. And then, a new groundskeeper had been hired. He and his eighteen-year-old daughter introduced themselves to Madison one morning with Stephen standing right next to her. When they walked away, Madison winked at Stephen. He'd seen it too, the way the daughter had looked at him in a flirty way. No girl had ever looked at him that way before, and he had only one person to thank for that.

2009

"Where the hell is Bernard?" George stood at the front door, briefcase in hand.

Madison looked around with concern. Bernard, their driver, always had the car waiting at 7:30 a.m. sharp. In her black business suit and heels, she followed her father across the pea gravel drive to the garages. They found Bernard talking to a young man who was sitting on a stool by the toolbox.

"What the hell, Bernard?" George looked at his watch. "Why don't you have the car ready and waiting? That's what I pay you for."

Bernard straightened his shoulders. "Sorry, sir." He glanced at the young man again. "I don't believe you've met my nephew. Stephen, this is Mr. Prescott and his daughter, Miss Madison."

Madison's eyes locked on the teenager with the black eye. "Hello, Stephen." He looked at her and nodded, then turned away.

"Get the damn car, Bernard."

George left the garage, but Madison walked farther in. She wanted to get a better look at the boy. She stood a few feet away and turned her attention to Bernard. "What's going on?"

"I'm so sorry, Miss Madison. He doesn't want to go to school today. I was trying to convince him."

"No. I don't suppose I'd want to go to school with a shiner like that, either."

Surprised by the response, Stephen glanced up at her, making eye contact.

"What happened, Stephen?"

He quickly shook his head. "It's no big deal."

"Bullies?" Madison put her hand up when Bernard tried to reply. She stared at Stephen until he finally nodded.

"He's new at school," Bernard explained, almost whispering. "You know how kids can be. Especially with the shy kids. And Stephen's so shy, he barely talks to me."

Madison walked over to Stephen. She lifted his chin so she could get a better look at his eye. It was swollen shut. "Let Bernard take you to the doctor today, okay?" Stephen nodded. "When do you graduate?"

"Hopefully, this year," Stephen said, his voice so low Madison had to strain to hear it.

"Hopefully?"

Bernard stepped a little closer. "He's trying hard. It's been a tough year."

Madison took a step back, her eyes going from Stephen to Bernard and back. "Stephen, I need my own driver now that I've started working in the city. I need someone responsible and dedicated and honest. Are you honest?"

Stephen stood up, his good eye suddenly full of hope. "Yes, Miss Madison."

"Good. I also need a high school graduate. So, focus on graduating, and I'll be there in the stands when you accept your diploma." She held out her hand. "Do we have a deal?"

Stephen's whole demeanor seemed to change. He stood a little taller and gave her a strong nod. "Yes, ma'am."

"Oh, and one other thing."

"Yes, Miss Madison?"

"Please don't call me Miss Madison. It sounds like the name of something they'd sell next to the Twinkies."

Stephen smiled. "Okay, Miss Prescott."

Madison sighed. "We'll work on the formalities later. In the meantime, you'd better get to school. Remember, if you let me down, I'll be stuck riding in with *King George* every day."

As if on cue, a bellow sounded in the distance. "Damn it, Bernard!"

Bernard and Stephen lowered their heads, trying not to smile. Madison rolled her eyes and turned to leave. "For the love of God, Stephen, don't let me down."

Present Day

Madison rested her head on Stephen's shoulder. "My mom was a good person like you, Stephen. I know she would've let me love Ana."

Stephen wasn't sure what to do. Something had changed in Madison since her father had died. She was letting it all hang out, so to speak, and Madison never did that. Never. She had always been so stoic, so reserved. She didn't laugh as much as he wished she would, and he had certainly never seen her cry. Now, the crying happened almost daily. Most of the time, it was just light sniffling he could hear behind him while driving, but still, he was starting to worry about her.

He prayed what he was about to do wouldn't be taken the wrong way. He couldn't bear it if he upset her even more. Gently, he put his arm around her shoulder and leaned in. Her head fell to his chest, and he leaned in farther, giving her support. "It's okay," he whispered, not sure he'd even said it loud enough for her to hear.

"Goddamn him," Madison said through her tears. "Goddamn that bastard."

Stephen handed her his handkerchief and held her for a long while. Several times, he moved to caress her hair but pulled his hand back, not sure what would be considered too much.

When he'd first started dating his wife, he had questions. He'd never had a girlfriend, never even been on a date. His Uncle Bernard had tried to answer most of them. Important things like, should Stephen start wearing cologne? Bernard said it couldn't hurt, but Madison got in the car one morning and within thirty seconds said, "Stephen, you don't want to smell better than your date. Why don't you buy a nice bottle of perfume for her instead of wearing it yourself?"

He'd probably overdone it with the cologne, but that was the day he'd stopped trusting Bernard and went straight to Madison for advice. With just a few words, she would make it crystal clear what his next move should be, and on his wedding day, she was there, in the front row, smiling from ear to ear.

When his daughter was born, Stephen had wondered what George would do if he asked Madison to be Kelsey's godmother. George was very unpredictable at times, firing people for no good reason. He might consider it an insult to his family since Stephen was just a driver. He might make a scene and kick him off of the property for being insolent like he'd done with the previous groundskeeper.

Stephen didn't want that for his new little family, but there really was only one person in this whole world he trusted enough to be there for his daughter if, God forbid, something was to happen to him.

He'd asked her in a letter. It was easier than trying to get the words out in person. He always stumbled over words—even ones that weren't weighed down by emotion. His new little baby meant the world to him. How could he possibly say out loud how strongly he felt about who her godmother should be? No, a letter was better. And that way, if Madison didn't want to say yes, she could say no in a letter too. And she wouldn't have to see Stephen's disappointment.

Madison hadn't said no. In fact, she'd arranged to have a beautiful brunch on the back veranda after the ceremony. Scott was there, but of course, George was nowhere to be found. He would never be seen mingling with his own staff, and Madison had invited everyone on the estate. These people were his family, Madison included. Next to his wedding day and Kelsey's birth, that day was far and away Stephen's proudest moment. He'd stood with his wife and his daughter in awe that so many people would celebrate his family.

Stephen would've stayed there all day on that bench, letting Madison cry for as long as she needed to. It was the intermittent raindrops that shortened the stay. Madison sat up and looked skyward. "Perfect," she said.

Stephen worked up the courage to say what was in his heart. "Ma'am," he whispered. "I'm always here for you. As your driver, but also—" He wanted to say, as a friend, but he averted his eyes and squeezed his hand into a fist.

"What, Stephen?" Madison wiped her nose with his handkerchief. "I just cried on your shoulder. I think that means you can say what's on your mind."

"I'm here for you, ma'am. As your driver and—" He patted his shoulder. "This, whenever you need it."

She put her hand on his knee. "Then for God's sake, stop calling me ma'am." She gave his knee a pat and stood up. "We're friends, Stephen. And don't you forget it."

CHAPTER TEN

Carmen insisted on paying for everything. She hadn't cashed in her newly acquired Prescott stock and probably never would, but she had a little nest egg she'd been saving in hopes she could one day throw her only child a proper wedding. Ana's social status certainly wouldn't allow for that now. Any wedding she and the good doctor had would require more than Carmen could afford. But she could afford a nice engagement party.

Carmen opted to have the party in Ana's home, rather than a restaurant. Even the nicest restaurant would most likely be crowded and noisy with servers interrupting conversations. Carmen wanted something more intimate where she could get to know Kris's friends and relatives. After all, they'd be family soon enough.

Ana had a long dining table that seated twelve and a big kitchen island to serve the food buffet style. There was plenty of seating in the living room as well. It would be perfect. Carmen was sure of it.

They'd invited fifteen people. Kris's parents, an aunt who lived in the city, and a few good friends from the hospital were all coming. On Ana's side, Carmen wasn't sure who was coming. She'd been coy about it, saying she'd invited a few friends from work. That was typical. Ana rarely gave details about her life, even to her own mother.

Carmen didn't even know about Kris until she'd caught them in bed together four months into their relationship. She knew better than to ask too many questions. Ana didn't react well when Carmen tried to push her on facts: things like, did she love Kris, or was this just a fling? Another woman she would eventually push away, or the woman of her dreams? Or both?

Carmen didn't really have to ask, though. She knew the answer before Ana had spoken a word. That's why she'd been so surprised by the news of the engagement. Surprised but happy. Maybe Ana had turned a corner in her life. Carmen hoped with all of her heart that it was true.

Ana rushed into the apartment. "Sorry, I'm late!" She pulled her sweater over her head as she ran into the bedroom.

Carmen just smiled. Everything was ready, and her daughter hadn't even noticed. She looked at her watch. *Thirty minutes and counting.*

Scott zipped up Madison's dress and rested his hands on her bare shoulders. "You look incredible." He met Madison's gaze in the mirror. "Absolutely gorgeous."

Madison wore a fitted, white sleeveless dress with a diamond solitaire necklace. Her hair was pulled up with a few strands loosely framing her face. "Why am I doing this to myself?"

"Because she invited us, honey. I know you would've preferred a simple lunch as a first step back to friendship, but you'll have to take whatever she's willing to give."

She knew Scott was right. It wasn't up to her how this would go. It had to be up to Ana. But Madison was nervous. "Albert's still out there."

"We'll find him. I have several guys working on it."

Madison tossed her lipstick in her clutch purse. "What the hell was I thinking, leaving Albert out there just blowing in the wind? If there's one thing George Prescott taught me, it's that you tie up loose ends."

"And we will, Maddy. Trust me on this one, okay?"

Madison scolded herself. It was sloppy, kicking Albert out like she had. She should've had better control of her emotions. All she could do now was hope and pray they'd find him before he did something stupid. She forced a smile, trying to pull herself out of the funk she'd been in since receiving the official invitation to Ana's engagement party. "You look smashing, as always. New suit?"

Scott ran his fingers through his thick black hair. He hadn't shaved in a few days, so he had a little salt and pepper stubble on his face. His new suit was a slimmer cut, complementing his long, lean body. "I thought I'd try a younger tailor. Joshua is too old to care about new trends. Do you think my hair is too long?"

Madison turned around and leaned on the sink so they were face-to-face. "Don't leave me alone with Ana tonight. I'll just end up in a pool of tears like last time."

Scott crossed his heart. "I swear."

Madison looked him over again. "I've always liked your hair a little longer."

"Your father hated it." He adjusted his cuffs. "Along with everything else about me."

"I think you're being harsh. He loved that you're a man." Madison smiled. "Besides, he's dead. Wear your hair however you like to wear it." She straightened his narrow black tie. "In fact, I think you should grow a beard."

Scott gasped. "Could you imagine George's reaction?"

"Yes." Madison grinned. "I can."

❖

"So glad you came." Ana air-kissed both Scott and Madison as if they were lifelong friends.

Madison's breath was taken away. Ana looked so beautiful in her slim-cut tuxedo pants, black heels, and a sparkly gold halter top that showed off her arms and shoulders.

Madison was surprised by the warm greeting. She'd expected a certain level of pleasantness, but Ana's greeting was downright affectionate. In fact, they still had hold of each other's hands when she said, "We wouldn't miss it."

She meant those words. After staring at the invitation for days, she handed it to Joss and asked her to send the RSVP. She would not, no matter how painful it might be, miss Ana's engagement party.

"Let me take your coat," Ana said. Madison didn't move. She was lost in the moment. Lost in the scent of Ana. Her voice. Her home. Madison was standing in Ana's home. It felt unreal.

Ana made a circling motion with her finger. "I can't take it off unless you turn around."

"Right. Sorry." Madison turned around and let her coat fall off of her shoulders. "Thank you," she whispered, catching Ana's eye.

She noticed Ana's eyes linger on her dress for a second before she took their coats to the closet. Carmen's eyes lit up when she saw her latest guests. "I had no idea you were coming! Welcome!" She hugged Madison and turned her attention to Scott. "And this is your husband, Maddy?"

"Scott, this is Ana's mother, Carmen. The woman who did so much for me when I was younger."

"Yes." Scott reached for Carmen's hand. "It's a pleasure to finally meet you, Carmen."

Carmen stepped closer and put her hand over Scott's. "Thank you for taking good care of her all these years."

Ana stepped up to them. She offered her guests a glass of champagne. "Let me introduce you to everyone." She led them into the living room where most of the guests were already snacking on hors d'oeuvres.

Madison followed, taking in every detail. Soft music was playing through speakers hidden in the white walls. She and Ana had similar tastes, leaning toward modern, but she already knew that. When they were young, they'd often talked about their future home and what it would look like. Ana had wanted a big bed. She'd lived her entire life in a twin-sized bed, knocking her knee against the wall one too many times. Madison doubted if she'd ever see the bedroom, but she had no doubt Ana had made that little dream come true.

"Scott! Oh my God!" One of Kris's friends came from across the living room and held out his hand. "You know Ana?" The stranger offered his hand to Madison as well. "Dave Osborne."

Madison took his hand and smiled. "Madison Prescott." She glanced at Scott, wondering if he'd left his manners in the car.

Scott cleared his throat and put his hand on Madison's lower back. "Dave, this is my wife. Maddy. Dave was the doctor who patched me up after that incident in Central Park."

Dave also cleared his throat. "Right. A loose dog, if I remember correctly."

"Jumped right out in front of me and knocked me on my ass, then tried to take a chunk out of my leg," Scott exclaimed, maybe a little too loudly. He took a large sip of champagne.

Ana took Madison's hand, holding it loosely. "Let's go before the details get too gory."

As they walked away, Madison heard Dave say, "I didn't know you were married." She turned back and glanced at Scott. He gave her a nervous smile.

Ana led Madison over to a table laden with hors d'oeuvres. She picked up a toast point covered in caviar. "Your favorite."

Madison's eyes sparkled with delight. "You remembered my favorite caviar?"

"How could I forget? I almost barfed the first time I tasted it."

Madison took a bite and hummed her delight. "So good."

Ana picked one up for herself and took a bite, causing Madison's eyes to widen in surprise. Ana shrugged. "I was fifteen. Show me a fifteen year old who appreciates good caviar. Besides you, of course."

"I developed my tastes early, I guess." Madison didn't mean to flirt, but it kind of came out that way with her gaze lingering on Ana's mouth.

Ana grabbed a napkin and took Madison's hand, wiping her finger clean. "Black caviar and that pretty white dress don't mix."

"No, I guess they don't." Madison watched Ana's every move. She should do the right thing and pull away, causing the electrical current that was so clearly flowing between them to collapse. But she couldn't. She needed this too much. She needed Ana's hands on her, even if it was just to wipe a little caviar from her finger.

❖

Carmen looked on in slight horror as Ana doted on Madison as if she was the only person in the room. Had her daughter completely lost her mind along with her manners? Had she really forgotten that Kris's family was there? Or Madison's husband?

She watched the two of them laugh about something, noticing how close they stood to one another. It had to stop. This was clearly inappropriate behavior, wasn't it? Or maybe it was only because she knew their history that Carmen could see it for what it was. No one else was turning bright red by the display. Carmen covered her neck with her hand, trying to hide her embarrassment. And that was all she would do because to do anything else would only put a wedge between her and Ana.

Finally, after an agonizingly long minute, one of Kris's friends walked up to Ana, causing Madison to take a step back. Carmen let out a long sigh of relief.

She began to wonder if Ana being on cloud nine for days before the party had anything at all to do with her fiancée. And she found herself feeling relieved that Kris had been delayed at the hospital and wasn't there to witness the blatant display of affection between the two women. Thank God for small blessings.

❖

Madison noticed a photograph on the wall. It was in a simple black frame with a large white mat surrounding the image. The photograph itself couldn't have been more than a 5x7, causing her to squint at it. She excused herself from the conversation and walked over to it, wanting a better look. She lost her breath for a moment when she realized what it was: a black and white photo of the big oak tree they'd climbed when they were kids. The same tree they were sitting under when Madison proposed to Ana.

She didn't know whether to be happy or sad that there was such a prominent reminder of their life together in Ana's home. Maybe there were still some good memories mixed in with the bad. She turned around, and Ana was right there, holding two glasses of champagne. "Care to get drunk with me?"

Madison took the glass. She wanted to comment on the photograph but thought better of it when Ana downed half of her glass in one swallow. "Where's your fiancée?"

"Um…" Ana looked around the apartment. "She's still not here?"

Madison chuckled. "I wouldn't know, Ana. What does she look like?" She wondered how many glasses of champagne Ana had consumed before they'd arrived.

"She's about my height, I guess. Where the hell is she? She said she was on her way."

Knowing that Kris wasn't there emboldened Madison. She knew it was wrong, but she couldn't help herself. She took a step closer and rested her hand on Ana's waist. The halter top didn't quite meet the waistband on the low-cut tuxedo pants, allowing her to graze Ana's bare skin with her thumb. "You look absolutely stunning tonight. Kris is a very lucky woman."

❖

George Prescott's longtime bodyguard and "fixer," entered the building and tipped his fedora at the doorman. "Good evening. I'm here for the engagement party. Ana Perez and Kris Armstrong?"

Albert knew the doorman had been waving people in all night. He would do the same with him, no questions asked. Some people just didn't take their jobs seriously enough. "Number 310," the doorman said, barely giving Albert a glance.

Albert removed his hat and smoothed out his graying mustache before he entered the apartment, holding a large envelope under his arm. The first person to see him was Carmen. He gave her a friendly nod and smiled when Madison turned his way. Ana was looking at him the way Carmen had, curious, but not entirely sure who he was. That wasn't a problem. He'd trimmed his hair and lost some weight. He was working out now. He'd cleaned up quite a bit. It'd been fifteen years. It made sense she didn't recognize him. She'd know soon enough.

Albert's view of the two gorgeous women who had obviously reconnected was suddenly obscured by Scott's tall form. "You make a better door than a window, Mr. Fairmont."

"We need to talk, Albert. Outside."

Albert didn't care much for Scott Fairmont. He couldn't respect a man who hadn't made his own way in the world. Madison's husband was one of those silver-spoon boys who had a position in his father's company but didn't actually work. Sure, he put on a suit and tie every day and rode into the city with Madison, sat at his desk for a few hours, and kissed the asses of their best clients by wining and dining them, but that wasn't real work. He was nothing more than a show pony with his good looks and winning smile.

Albert brushed Scott's hand off of his shoulder. "There's no need to put your hands on me, son."

"Oh God." Carmen covered her mouth with her hand.

Albert gave her another nod. "It's nice to finally be remembered, Carmen. You're looking well."

"Let me handle this," Madison said with Ana right behind her.

He nodded an acknowledgment to them as they walked up. "Now that we're all here, why don't we find somewhere to talk?" He turned and smiled at Carmen. "You too, Carmen."

Madison stepped in front of Ana, blocking her way. "Do you mind if we talk to Albert somewhere private? Do you have an office or a guest bedroom?"

Ana ignored Madison and glared at the man. "I remember you. You're the man who kicked us off of the estate. You broke our TV. You called me a—"

Madison took Ana by the arm and pulled her away from the group. "Just let me handle this. You stay here and entertain your guests. Please, Ana."

"*All* of you," Albert said. "Including Ana." He noticed a hallway and headed for it, opening the first door he found. "This will do," he said, waving them into the room. They all walked into the master suite, and Scott closed the door behind them.

"What the hell is going on?" Ana looked around at everyone, waiting for an answer.

"Albert." Madison stepped forward. "I'm sure we can work this out in the office tomorrow. I was a bit hasty when I—"

"When you kicked me out? Hell, you owed me one. Can't say what happened to Carmen and Ana that day was one of my prouder moments, but it wasn't the worst thing I've ever done either. I was a terrible, pathetic drunk whose only redeeming quality was the check your father sent to my ex-wife and kid every month. That's how he got me. Whatever kind of mess I was in, I always knew they'd be okay." Albert sighed. "Since Mr. Prescott died, I've had a lot of time to think."

Scott stepped forward. "Albert, whatever this is about—"

"I'm here to make things right," Albert said, interrupting him. "I'm also here to declare my loyalty to you, Madison. That's not what Mr. Prescott would've wanted, but he's six feet under now, thanks to you and Ana." He shrugged. "I'm good at making myself invisible when I need to be, but I was there, watching the two of you. It gave me pause, to say the least."

"Albert, please," Madison said. "This is an engagement party you're interrupting."

"I'm very aware of what's going on. And I'll get to that in a minute. First, I need to know if you accept my offer of loyalty. I won't ask you to accept my apology for the part I played in keeping the two of you apart. Just accept my offer of loyalty. That's all I ask."

Madison looked at Ana, then nodded. "Okay, Albert. If it'll mean we can get back to the party sooner."

Albert took two envelopes out of his coat pocket. "I wasn't going for theatrics by showing up this way. I just needed all of you in the same room so that the lies could stop." He held up the first envelope. "These are my instructions from Mr. Prescott. I'm to use any means necessary to keep you two apart, aside from physically hurting you, Madison. But we both know that any physical pain you have or will suffer is the least of it."

Ana looked at Madison. "What is he talking about?"

Albert held up the other envelope. "I was just about to get to that." He turned his attention to Carmen. "Or maybe your mother would like to be the one to tell you about *El Serpiente*. Either way, you should know the truth before you marry Dr. Armstrong."

Kris opened the door. She eyed everyone in the room, then walked up to Ana and kissed her cheek. "Sorry, I'm late."

"Well, well," Albert said. "Kris Armstrong, doctor extraordinaire. Mr. Prescott had such high hopes for you, but you just couldn't seem to close the deal. That is, until now, of course."

Ana narrowed her eyes at him. "How do you know Kris? And who the hell is *El Serp*—whatever?"

"There isn't much I don't know about you, Ana" Albert said. "Mr. Prescott was especially pleased with your latest choice. He really wanted it to work out for you."

"Albert, I think you've said enough for one night." Scott kissed Ana's cheek. "We're so sorry for the interruption. Please, accept our heartfelt congratulations."

Scott stood between Albert and the two women. He motioned for Albert to follow them, but had Albert said enough? He wasn't sure. Madison walked up to him and held out her hand. She wanted the envelopes. Maybe this wasn't the best move after all. And maybe redemption and forgiveness were just words.

Albert wasn't sure what his next move should be. All he knew was that his AA sponsor couldn't stop talking about honesty and making amends. It seemed like a bunch of hooey at first, but lately it was starting to make sense. Especially when he thought about Madison and Ana.

Ana had a right to know what had really kept her and Madison apart for all of those years before she married someone she didn't really love. He'd kept close tabs on Ana and Kris's relationship for Mr. Prescott. He knew how up and down it was. It made him sad that Ana hadn't ever really been able to move on from Madison. And seeing them in the same room together now, he knew without a doubt the damage he'd done by following Mr. Prescott's orders without question all those years.

He knew revealing who Ana's father was would be another devastating blow to Ana's heart, but keeping the secret would be even worse, wouldn't it? *Be part of the solution, not the problem.* He could hear his sponsor's voice in his head as he handed the envelopes to Madison.

Madison took the envelopes and turned to Ana. "I'll take care of this," she said.

"Take care of what, Maddy? What's going on?"

Carmen stepped forward and held out her hand for one of the envelopes. "Let me be the one to tell her."

❖

Madison stood when Carmen walked into the coffee shop. She kissed her cheek and gave her a hug. "Tell me everything."

Carmen sat and took off her coat. "The short answer is the engagement is on hold, and Ana hates her mother now."

"I'm sure that's not true."

"She screamed at me for lying to her about her father all of those years. I was worried her neighbors would call the police."

"It's understandable that she would be upset," Madison said. "Maybe she just needs some time to process it."

"It's more than that." Carmen took a tissue out of her coat pocket and dabbed her swollen eyes. "Every day, Ana calls me to check in. Without fail. But I haven't heard from her in four days."

Madison's calls had gone unanswered as well. That's why she'd asked Carmen to meet her. She was also going crazy with worry, but she tried not to show it. "Can't you call her at work? Surely, her assistant would put you through to her."

"No," Carmen said. "She took a leave of absence from work, and no one has seen or heard from her since."

Madison didn't want to ask what she feared most—that Ana would contact her father. Then, she realized she didn't have to ask. Carmen was thinking the same thing. She could see it in her eyes. "Carmen."

"God help us, Maddy." Carmen wrung her hands together. "He'll find me, and he'll kill me if he finds out about her."

"I don't think Ana would risk that. No matter how badly she wants to know her father." Madison reached for Carmen's hand.

"I have resources. I have…I have Albert. Tell me what to do, Carmen. It's up to you."

"Albert," Carmen scoffed. She shook her head in disgust. "I don't trust that man." She took another tissue out of her pocket and dabbed her nose.

Madison understood better than anyone how hard it would be to put any faith in Albert. She just prayed he wasn't just trying to keep his job, but that he really wanted to redeem himself in their eyes. Only time would tell. In the meantime, she wanted to keep him in her line of sight.

"Did you bring it?" Carmen asked.

"Yes." Madison reached into her pocket and pulled out the envelope Albert had given her. "You don't need to read this to know what an awful man my father was. Maybe it's best not to."

Carmen took the envelope and pulled out the letter. She read it and then looked out the window for a moment. "It's as if this was a game to him. Something fun he did on the weekends. Getting his weekly reports about my daughter's comings and goings and then smoking a cigar in the library, feeling so pleased with himself that he'd kept you two apart."

"If it gives you any comfort, just know that all of his spying was for nothing," Madison said. "I never would've risked Ana's safety by going anywhere near her." She lowered her head for a moment as her emotions bubbled to the surface. "I think you're right. I think he reveled in his achievement. And I think he knew what you knew, Carmen—that I would run to Ana as soon as he took his last breath."

Carmen folded the letter and put it back in the envelope. She slid it across the table and said, "Tell Albert to find Ana before she does something stupid."

CHAPTER ELEVEN

2003

Madison contemplated abandoning the long line that didn't seem to be moving. Maybe the espresso machine was broken again. She was just about to leave her favorite coffee shop when she was yanked out of the line and pulled into the bathroom. Ana locked the door and turned around. "What the hell is going on?"

Madison blinked. And then blinked again. "Oh God. God, I miss you." She fell into Ana's arms and held on tight.

Ana tried to pull out of the hug. "Maddy, what's going on? You were supposed to meet me at the hotel, and then I got this crazy text. Why haven't you answered my phone calls? I've been worried sick."

Madison let go. "I can't. We can't."

"Why not? Is it George? What did he do this time?"

Madison remembered the picture of *El Serpiente*. Looking into Ana's eyes now, she could see the resemblance. There was no doubt that Ana was that awful man's daughter. She pulled her close again and kissed her cheek. "I love you, Ana. Don't ever forget that." She opened the door and rushed out of the coffee shop.

"You can't say that, Maddy, and then just walk away. You owe me an explanation!" Ana's voice echoed through the parking lot. They could so easily make a plan, couldn't they? Maybe meet at another hotel, far from town? Madison scanned the parking lot to see if she recognized any cars. Was Albert on her tail? She couldn't know for sure. She wanted to tell Ana again how much she loved her. How miserable she'd been without her. How her life was only worth living if she was in it. Her stomach retched, but she kept walking. There wasn't anything in it anyway, since she hadn't been able to eat anything of substance for days.

Ana got in front of her and blocked her from her car. "You have to talk to me, Maddy. I'm dying without you."

Madison felt as if she was dying too. All she wanted to do was lie in Ana's arms again. Feel her warmth, hear her sweet giggle, kiss her soft lips, and say the thing she'd said a thousand times before—*You're mine, Ana. You'll always be mine.* But she couldn't risk it. "You have to believe me when I tell you that if I had a choice—"

Ana grabbed Madison's shoulders. "You *do* have a choice. We run. Right now. Just get the hell out of this town and drive until we run out of gas. He doesn't own you, Maddy. Those are your words. You've been telling me that for years. He doesn't own you."

"He would find us. He would ruin us. I can't let that happen."

Ana pulled back a little. "So, it was all just a lie? You and me, finding a life for ourselves, far away from him? Throw a dart on a map? Isn't that what you said?" Ana's voice cracked. "Maddy, look at me."

Madison couldn't. She kept her head down and tried to hold back the tears. She had to be strong now, for Ana's sake.

"God, how could I have been so stupid to think you'd give it all up for me? Was I just a game for you, Maddy?"

Madison shook her head. "No. You were—" *Everything. My life. My heart.*

Ana pulled the chain out from under her shirt that held her engagement ring. "You asked me to marry you. Do you remember that, Maddy? You asked, and I said yes."

Madison couldn't take it anymore. Her heart was breaking in two, but she couldn't let Ana see that. She'd had to face the fact that her father held all the cards, and her ability to choose her own path in life had vanished. She had to protect Ana. Above all else, she had to protect Ana, even if it meant hurting her for a little while.

Ana would get over it. She'd move on and find love eventually. The thought of Ana being with someone else tore Madison apart so much that she couldn't hold back the tears anymore. She quickly wiped them away and told the biggest lie she'd ever tell—the only lie Ana might believe. "I'm a Prescott, Ana. And Prescotts don't marry the maid's daughter."

The words took all of the air from Madison's lungs. She was so disgusted that she'd used her father's own words to destroy Ana's heart that she wanted to bend over and vomit. A deep sob found its way up as she whispered, "I'm sorry."

Ana didn't move. Her mouth hung open as tears filled her eyes. After a painfully long moment of silence, she pulled the chain over her head and held it out.

Madison wanted to scream. She wanted to take it all back and push Ana into her car and drive until they found an ocean. She would beg for Ana's forgiveness and kiss away her tears and tell her about—her father? *El Serpiente*? No. She couldn't do that. It would destroy Ana, and then Madison's own father would come and finish the job.

Madison took the necklace with her grandmother's ring attached from Ana's hand. She wondered how anyone could destroy the girl they loved and still recover? How would either of them ever move on from such a betrayal? Madison wasn't religious, but she promised herself that she'd pray every day for Ana to find a way. *Move on, Ana. Forget you ever knew me. Be happy.*

Present Day

"Your mother is worried sick about you."

Ana didn't acknowledge the person who had just plopped down in the sand next to her. She casually closed the journal she'd been writing in and put the lid back on the pen. It was true she hadn't contacted her mother since she'd stormed out of her apartment the night of the infamous engagement party.

Learning who her father really was and that her mother had been lying to her about him her entire life had been a devastating blow to their relationship. The following morning, she'd asked her company for a leave of absence and quickly left town. They couldn't really say no since she hadn't taken a single day off in two years.

Nothing made sense to Ana anymore. The battle she'd fought to make something of herself and make her parents proud was a battle fought in vain. She was and always would be the daughter of Vincent Villareal, also known as *El Serpiente*—a man who had followed in his father's footsteps, becoming one of the most powerful and most feared men in Mexico. What good would it do to work as hard as she had when it could all so quickly be taken from her if Albert or anyone else made the truth known to the world? Her career would be over. No one would ever hire her to oversee their investments.

Ana had to wonder what other landmines George had planted before his death. Would her world explode right in front of her when she least expected it? The man seemed to hate her with a passion, so it wouldn't surprise Ana if he made good on his threats post-mortem. It seemed she was destined to live her life in fear. Always running from her past. Always running from love.

Ana lifted her sunglasses and wrapped her arms around her legs to keep her long skirt from billowing in the breeze. "You're not really dressed for the beach."

Madison chuckled and took her suit jacket off, revealing a white, sleeveless blouse. "Is that better?"

Ana shook her head. "Not really. You still look like a flight attendant who has stopped caring. One too many flights to paradise, so fuck it. I'm sitting my ass down in the sand in this navy-blue pantsuit." She hid her amusement. Madison looked stunning, as always, but insults were easier.

"I'm never wearing it again if that's what I look like." Madison tossed the jacket aside and glanced at Ana's arms. "Remember how tanned you would get in the summer and how I would stay the same pasty shade of white?"

"You'd get so many freckles on your nose." A smile crept in. Ana quickly suppressed it. "But, yeah. You were the white girl and I was the—" It wasn't a fair comment. Ana knew that Madison never cared about their differences. Madison was staring at her, waiting for her to finish. "Why are you here? I mean, I've always had a thing for flight attendants, but you're a married woman."

"Flight attendants? Really?"

Madison looked so serious, Ana wanted to laugh out loud. Did she really want to know her "type"? Madison probably wanted to know everything. Every little detail about who Ana had become. How many girlfriends she'd had. That wasn't happening. "The truth has never mattered to you, but if you must know, I like anyone whose name doesn't start with M. I don't date Mollys or Marias or Madelines."

Madison scowled at her. She made a move to get up but stopped. "It's time to go home, Ana. Or at least call your mom. She's barely hanging in there without you."

"You came all this way to tell me my mother is worried about me? Did you also come to tell me all the lies were for my own good?"

Madison shot her a glare. "I came because I promised her I'd find you and bring you back."

"That's a pretty big promise. Of course, you always were one for making promises you couldn't keep." Ana picked up her journal and stood. "Whatever. You're all a bunch of damn liars. Every last one of you."

"You don't know the threats my father made. You have no idea," Madison said.

"I don't care what threats he made," Ana shouted. "You didn't trust me with the truth. First my mother and then *you* decided what was best for me, taking away *any* choice I had."

"So, what was I supposed to do?" Maddy shouted back. "Just let my dad ruin your life? I couldn't do that. I loved you too much. I still love you!"

Just as Ana had always known—love meant nothing. It was just a word. "Go home, Maddy. There's nothing left to say."

Madison's face reddened with anger. "You think you're the only one who lost something? The only one who was lied to? He threatened to plant drugs in your dorm room, Ana. He said he would ruin your credit, your job prospects, your entire future! I *had* to toe the line! For *you*, Ana. I toed the fucking line for fifteen years! Does that not mean *anything* to you?"

Ana didn't have an answer. All she knew for sure was that when she looked at Madison, she saw a liar. And that thought brought up another issue. "How did you find me? Albert? The man who apparently knows more about me than I know about myself?"

Madison softened her tone. "You used your debit card. Surely, you knew—"

Ana chuckled. "God, Maddy. You think I wanted to be found?"

"Didn't you?"

"I don't even know how I can go back home. I feel so violated by him. I'm scared to take a shower in my own home for fear he's watching me. I haven't used a phone since I left. I haven't checked my email or talked to anyone close to me. And yeah, I used my debit card because I desperately needed a coffee and didn't have any cash on me. The fact that you know that just proves my point."

"I'll shut it down," Madison said. "Whatever surveillance he was doing, you have my word, it will stop. I'll call someone and have them check your home for cameras and bugs. I'll give you a bodyguard if that would make you feel better. Whatever you need."

Ana shook her head in disgust. "Why didn't you shut it down the second you found out about it? And how *dare* you use the same man that threw us out of our home to find me now! God, Madison, have you no shame?"

Madison grabbed Ana's arm. "Your mother was desperate to find you. And whether we like it or not, Albert is less of a threat if we keep him close."

"Stop saying *we*! There is no *we*! Albert is *your* problem, but so help me God, if I ever see his face again…"

"You won't," Madison said. "You have my word."

"Your word." Ana almost laughed. "Tell me a time when your word meant anything, Maddy."

Madison stiffened. "I'll let your mom know you're okay."

"You do that," Ana snapped back. "And just so we're clear, my mother may be for sale, but I'm not. You can't just throw money around and expect me to forget what you did to me."

"That's not why she got the stock, and you know it."

Ana's eyes narrowed. She lunged toward Madison, stopping just short of touching her. "Did it ease your conscience, Maddy? Did it erase what you and your father did to us? And how does it feel right now, knowing that I still hate you, 1.5 million dollars later?"

Madison's jaw flexed. "Hate is a big word, Ana. It sure didn't feel like you hated me at your engagement party. In fact, I think for a minute there, you forgot you even had a fiancée."

"Fuck you." Ana pushed Madison away, making her stumble backward in the sand.

Madison righted herself and went back for more. "You forgot, didn't you? You took one look at me and forgot who you were going to marry."

"Don't talk to me about marriage, Maddy. You of all people."

"Oh, I'm exactly the person who should talk to you about marriage because I know what it looks like when you're marrying someone you're not in love with. And you, Ana, are not in love with Kris. You're in love with the idea of Kris because she's a successful doctor, and your mom loves her, and she's everything you think you need, but you're wrong."

Ana folded her arms. "So, what does the *great* Madison Prescott think I need?"

Madison's eyes filled with tears. She blinked them away. "Me. You need me."

Ana's eyes widened. "You're married, Maddy. Or have you forgotten?" Madison looked away. "Oh," Ana said. "You meant as a friend. Yeah, for a stupid minute, I thought we could be friends. In fact, that's why I invited you to my engagement party, to start that process. But we can't *be* just friends, Maddy. We never could. Even when we were little, we were more than friends. We were soulmates. We took care of each other. We nurtured each other's spirit. We were everything. And then, you and your father tore my world apart. You ripped my heart out of my chest and stomped on it. And it still hasn't recovered. I'm still a fucking disaster when it comes to loving someone. I can't give them all of me because I'm so fucking scared they'll decimate me the way you did." Ana walked away.

"Do you understand that I had to protect you, Ana?" Madison caught up to her. "Please, tell me you know that protecting you was my only motive."

Ana gave her an incredulous look. "It seemed to serve you pretty well too. I mean, you have George's company now. And the estate. And more money than you could ever spend."

"And I would've gladly given it all up to spend my life with you."

Ana stopped. "Would you still?"

"I don't have to. He's dead, Ana. And why would you even ask that of me? Haven't we both lost enough?"

"I lost *everything*," Ana shouted, grateful they were on an empty, windy beach at dusk. "My *mom* lost everything. We had to scratch our way back up. I worked my ass off to get where I am today. I'm *still* working my ass off. So, tell me, Maddy, tell me one thing you lost."

"No, you're right." Sarcasm dripped from Madison's voice. "I didn't lose anything the day I walked away from you. Absolutely nothing, Ana. You really never meant that much to me. And when I asked you to marry me, I really only wanted to see if you'd say yes. Is that what you want to hear? Will that make you feel even a little more justified in your hatred?"

"Hey, at least you remember that we were engaged. I figured you'd blocked that from your mind and pretended it never happened."

"I've never forgotten that," Madison said. "I've remembered it every day for fifteen years." Madison turned and tried to walk away, but Ana grabbed her arm.

"Don't you dare walk away from me!"

"And don't you dare pretend that my heart didn't break into just as many pieces as yours did. You really think I could just forget that I put my grandmother's ring on your finger?" Madison grabbed Ana by the shoulders. "I remember everything. Every touch. Every kiss. Every dream we dreamed. And shame on you for *still* believing that my love for you was somehow less than yours. That my pain was in *any* way numbed with money. Goddamn you for thinking me so shallow, after everything we meant to each other."

Ana stood motionless as Madison walked away.

❖

Madison didn't regret the decision she'd made fifteen years ago. She did the right thing. She knew it in her heart, and she couldn't take it back or even apologize for it. The fact that Ana would never understand was a painful reality and one Madison couldn't seem to do anything about. Ana's heart was too closed off to see anything but her own pain.

Madison got on the elevator and leaned against the wall. She closed her eyes and took a deep breath. She'd call Carmen when she got to the room and let her know that Ana was fine. Angry as hell, but fine.

"Thanks," Ana said.

Madison opened her eyes. Ana got on the elevator behind a young couple. She leaned against the opposite wall and met Madison's stare. The young couple leaned against the back wall. The giggling and kissing made Madison think they were on their honeymoon.

"Is your marriage real?"

The young couple froze, then looked at Madison and waited for an answer to Ana's question.

"Your marriage, Maddy. Is it real? Because I've been putting two and two together—"

The doors opened, and the couple rushed out. Madison wanted to rush out too, but she'd have to walk up ten flights of stairs.

"Your friend at Yale," Ana said. "The guy you studied with who you thought was gay—that's Scott, right?

Madison twisted the ring on her finger. She wanted to take it off and throw it at the wall; that's how little it meant to her. It wasn't Ana's ring. She would've given her entire inheritance to wear Ana's ring. She nodded. "Yes."

The doors opened. Madison's chest heaved as she walked down the hall. She'd done what she had to do. She pledged her life to someone else in the hope her father would let Ana be happy and successful in her own right. It had worked. But Madison felt the pain of that moment all over again when she'd said *I do* to someone who wasn't Ana. She pulled her key card from her front pocket.

Ana caught up to her in the hall. "So, you married him, knowing he was gay?"

Madison slid the card into the lock and opened her door. "That's *why* I married him. It worked for both of us. It served a purpose." She went straight for the mini bar.

Ana closed the door behind them and walked into the suite. "So, all this time. All this fucking time, I thought you'd stopped loving me because I wasn't good enough or rich enough or white enough. And you just let me believe that?"

Madison poured vodka into a glass and threw it back in one swallow. "It was the only thing you'd believe. It was the only way I could keep you away from me."

"Fabulous," Ana said in a sarcastic tone. "But you still haven't answered the question. Is your marriage real?"

"Can I get you a drink?" Madison grabbed two more bottles out of the fridge.

"Do you or don't you have sex with your husband?"

"Sex isn't the most important thing."

"Well," Ana said. "That's certainly not how the girl I remember felt about it. As I recall—"

"Stop," Madison said. She knew she would lose this argument. Sex had been something they both loved. And they hadn't let the lack of privacy stop them. They had sex in cars, on small dorm room beds, behind the horse stables on the estate. To pretend that it hadn't been as important as it was seemed wrong. She looked Ana in the eye. "Why are you suddenly so interested in my marriage?"

"You left me for him. I think I have a right to know."

Madison opened another bottle. "We have an agreement." She poured it into her glass, then stilled when Ana stepped closer.

"Have you ever acted on that agreement?"

Madison didn't answer. She went to pick up the glass, but Ana put her hand on it. She breathed in Ana's perfume and turned her head slightly, keeping her eyes down. "No," she whispered.

"And you're not in love with him?"

"I love him," Madison said. "But we're not in love."

Ana took her hand off of the glass, but she didn't step back. "That means I'm still the only one."

With every word, Ana's voice had softened. Madison wanted to trust this, but just minutes ago, Ana had so much rage in her eyes, she looked as if she wanted to kill her. Madison turned so they were face-to-face. "What do you want, Ana?"

Ana took a step back.

"Don't." Madison grabbed her hand. "Tell me. what do you want."

"I want what was taken from me," Ana said.

❖

The second the words came out of her mouth, Ana found herself regretting them. This was all wrong. The fire between them was burning as hot as ever. Whatever happened would be passionate and angry and sad and…not how Ana had imagined it. There was too much pain. Too much sorrow that even mind-blowing sex couldn't mask.

Could it be true, though? Could Madison really have stayed in a loveless marriage for so long? The thought broke Ana's heart. "I thought you loved him. I didn't know."

"I do love him," Madison said. "But I've never been in love with him."

"You said that already." Ana took a tentative step closer. Would it be cruel to take Madison into her arms, or would she consider it a gift? A cruel gift, maybe? Because then what? Would they make love in this hotel room and then go back to their very separate lives? Would they find a way to be together?

Ana didn't have the answers, but the pull was intense, and being even closer to Madison felt necessary. She touched her cheek and let a thumb brush her lips. "What am I going to do with you," she whispered.

Madison mimicked her action. She touched Ana's cheek and said, "If I were you, I'd kiss me."

Ana took Madison's face in her hands. "What if I die from heartache all over again?"

"I won't let that happen."

It was everything, kissing Madison again. Her hands were right where they had always been, clinging to Ana's waist. Her kiss was soft and tender and oh so familiar. Ana deepened the kiss, and Madison's hands moved lower, gripping her hips.

A fire burned inside of Ana that she hadn't felt in a very long time. The longer they kissed, the more she realized they were getting closer to the point of no return. Clothes would come off soon, and Madison would be naked and writhing underneath her. Ana wanted it so badly. She wanted to hear all the words Madison used to say when they made love. *I love you. Forever. You and me. Forever.*

But words meant nothing.

Ana broke the kiss and held Madison's forehead to her own until she caught her breath. "You should've found a way." She let go and took a step back. "You should have found a way, Maddy."

"What? Ana, no."

Madison reached for her, but Ana backed away. "No, Maddy. We should've had this all along. If you really loved me—"

Madison's stare hardened. "Why can't you see that everything I did, every decision I made, was for you?"

"I would've fought for you. For us! God, Maddy. You just walked away and never looked back."

"Every day." Madison put her hands over her mouth as tears came to her eyes. "I looked back every single day."

Ana shook her head in disbelief. She backed away and turned for the door. She put her hand on the handle and turned back around. "I would've fought like hell for you." She left the room and stopped short when she heard her name being yelled through the door. It wouldn't do any good to turn around. The passion was still there, but the trust was gone. And it always would be.

CHAPTER TWELVE

S cott poked his head in Madison's room. "You awake?"
Madison set her book on her lap and patted the bed. "Come in. Sit down."

"Thanks for making it on time for dinner." Scott sat on the edge of the bed. "I know celebrating my parent's wedding anniversary isn't high on your list of priorities right now."

"I'm sorry I've been so busy lately."

"Everything okay?"

Nothing was okay. It had been weeks since she and Ana had fought on that beach in California. She hadn't told Scott about what had happened in her hotel room after the beach. Even though the intimate moment with Ana had been fraught with anger and frustration, it had also been an awakening for Madison. She'd pushed those feelings so far down, she'd forgotten what it felt like to really connect with another human being.

Ana had reignited something inside of her. Something that she didn't want to run away from. She wanted to feel it, bask in it, have more of it in her life again.

"Maddy?"

"Yeah." Madison laid her head back against the headboard. "I was just thinking about the kids we never had."

"We agreed we didn't want them."

"We agreed we didn't want my dad raising our child." Madison sighed deeply. "How can one man ruin so many lives?"

Scott put his hand on her knee. "It's not too late to really live, Maddy. If a child is what you want, we could make that happen."

"Is that what you want?"

"I…" Scott hesitated. "You saved me from a life of loneliness and heartache. My family and everyone I knew would've disowned me if they'd known I was gay. Instead, I got to live my life married to a beautiful woman who truly loves me unconditionally." He paused. "Anyway, a night like tonight, with my parents, never would've happened without you. So, whatever you want is exactly what I'll give you."

The words sounded good, but Madison sensed tension in Scott's voice. "You can be very sweet when you're not answering a question."

"There are no easy answers."

They hadn't talked about children in a very long time. Madison wasn't even sure why the subject was weighing so heavily on her mind. Maybe it was just the turmoil George's death had caused in her life. Maybe it was knowing she'd never have what she'd always hoped for—to have Ana back in her life. Whatever the reason, she was feeling the huge void that the loss of her only real family had left. She hated George, but he was still her father.

"You know, it'd be pretty funny if we had a kid." Scott grinned. "After all those years of telling George how hard we were trying? I mean, how much time do you think we spent going to fake fertility appointments?"

Madison covered her eyes in embarrassment. "Oh my God. I don't even want to know. You realize your parents would die, right?"

"My parents? What about my brother? The poor bastard had to churn out four of them just to keep my parents happy."

"Oh please. Your brother adores those kids. Well, three of them, at least. Lisa, I'm not so sure about."

Scott chuckled. "Yeah, we probably should have had one kid just so I could've avoided that Thanksgiving when your dad got drunk and told everyone I have a low sperm count because of my tight pants. As if my little guys couldn't get the job done. God, your father really was an asshole."

"That's true. He really was an asshole." Madison looked away for a moment and then said, "Scott?"

"Yes?"

"I may have told George your sperm count was low to get him off my back."

Scott gasped in mock horror and threw a pillow at her. "I hate you. You realize that, right?"

Madison laughed and threw the pillow back at him. Until now, she hadn't had the courage to ask about the man she'd met at the engagement party well over a month ago. She wasn't blind. It was obvious they had some sort of connection, but it was the first time she'd met someone Scott had been with. "Tell me about Dave."

Scott took a deep breath and then slowly blew it out. "Wow. Okay, but just so you know, there haven't been that many guys. I know you said I could live my life, but honestly, Maddy, there haven't been that many. Dave was…I really liked him, so I took a chance. And I seriously wanted to leave that party the second I saw him. You have to know I never wanted to put you in that position."

"I know." Madison wanted Scott to feel as if he could talk about it. Dave seemed so happy to see him again; she'd wondered if another heart had been broken. "He seemed nice. A little short for you but nice."

Scott laughed. "Yeah. We'd be an odd couple, that's for sure." He shook his head. "Not a couple. You know what I mean."

Madison reached for his hand. "It's okay. I'm glad you found someone you like."

Scott put his hand over hers. "I'm sorry things haven't worked out with Ana. I know what she means to you."

Madison leaned back against the headboard again. "Some things can't be fixed once they're broken."

❖

Ana had thrown herself back into her work after the abysmal beach encounter with Madison. She worked late into the evening most nights and tried not to think about how fucked up her personal life had become.

She'd told Kris that she was in no position emotionally to even think about getting married. What she really needed to do was tell her it was over. Ana wasn't in love with Kris. She knew that now.

It was after six p.m. when security called up to her office telling her Scott Fairmont was there to see her. She hesitated. What the hell did he want? She decided she'd rather know than not know.

She was standing outside of her office waiting for him when he turned the corner. Scott Fairmont was statuesque, if you could describe a man that way. He wore a black overcoat and sunglasses. His dark hair was slicked back. Ana thought his beard seemed thicker. It was a good look on him, she supposed. He walked toward her with confidence and offered his hand. "Ana. Thank you for seeing me."

Ana motioned for him to join her in the office and then closed the door. "What can I do for you, Scott?"

Scott took off his overcoat and laid it over the arm of a chair. "Two things. Number one, I didn't get a chance to say it at the party, but you're just as beautiful as Maddy said you were. And number two, I need to know what your intentions are as far as Madison is concerned."

Ana was totally thrown. She wanted to hate Scott Fairmont, but he was nothing like she'd imagined him to be. He was confident but not arrogant. And he had kind eyes. She hadn't noticed that at the engagement party. Of course, she'd only had eyes for Madison that night. "I'm not sure what you're asking."

"May I sit?"

"Of course." He was so polite; he wouldn't even sit down until Ana had. She chose to sit behind her desk, needing the distance.

"I think enough has happened between all of us that we can be candid with one another."

"How refreshing," Ana replied with a slight tone of sarcasm in her voice. "Does that mean you're not going to lie to me and call it love? Because that's what everyone else seems to do."

"Quite the opposite, actually. I'm going to tell you everything I know and try to answer any questions you might have. And then, you're going to tell me if I should divorce Madison."

Ana couldn't hold his stare. Should he divorce Madison? *What the actual fuck?* She picked up a paperclip and twirled it between two fingers, something she did when she was trying to solve a problem. Having someone willing to tell her the whole truth without concern for her feelings was appealing. The last part was confusing. "Why would I tell you what to do, Scott?"

"Sometimes, when you love someone as much as I love Madison, you have to do what's right for them, even if it means letting them go."

Ana dropped the paperclip and gave him a dark stare. "Maybe that's what the Prescotts and the Fairmonts do, but in my world, you fight for the people you love. You don't, as you say, let them go."

"Sometimes, fighting for the one you love means letting them go."

Words. God, Ana was so sick of fancy phrases that meant absolutely nothing. The world was full of them. Everywhere she went, some stupid saying about love was plastered on a wall or a dishtowel. She'd even seen them on bar napkins, of all places. Scott's words reminded her of that one about letting someone go, and if they come back, they were always yours. Such fucking bullshit.

"You know, Scott, I'm really not interested in hearing how Madison did the right thing by throwing me away all those years ago."

"I wasn't talking about Madison." Scott leaned forward in his chair. "The only way to make you understand is to start at the beginning. The day Madison proposed and you said yes was the happiest day of her life. She was much braver than I was. She didn't want to hide that she was gay. She wanted to shout it to the world. But the day she lost you—Ana, I've never seen anyone like that before, so sad and broken. I wanted to kill her father for what he'd done."

"So, you knew about my real dad? The threats George made?"

Scott shook his head. "No. She didn't tell me the details. She just said he would ruin you and your mother's life. But I knew the man, so I knew however bad I might have imagined the circumstances, it was probably ten times worse. I only learned about your real father shortly before you did."

Ana remained still in her chair. The fact that Scott had been in the dark about her father, just like she had been, was a relief. It was silly to feel that way, but there was some comfort there. She'd take it.

"Look," Scott said. "I know you probably have a lot to do. I'll try to condense this—"

"No," Ana interrupted. "You can slow down. I don't have anywhere I need to be."

Scott relaxed a little in his chair, loosening his tie. "Thank you. There's so much you don't know, but if you want to know, I'd love to tell you."

Ana didn't know where to start, so she just started at the beginning. Or the end, depending on how she looked at it. "Why don't you tell me how Miss Prescott became Mrs. Fairmont?"

"It was my idea," Scott said. "You might have figured it out by now, or maybe Dave told you, but I'm gay too. And so, the marriage helped both of us. At school, we spent every possible minute together anyway because Maddy was so sad, and I was so scared, you know?" Scott shook his head. "I guess you don't know."

"When in doubt, it's safe to assume I didn't know. Anything." Ana picked up the paperclip again. "Please, tell me the rest."

"Anyway, the Madison we all knew and loved—that brilliant, kind, happy, secure person—disappeared for a while. For a long while. Long after we were married, even. In fact, I don't think she ever fully recovered. But somehow, we made a life together. We got through it. We had a wing in the estate; we both worked hard, she for her dad and me for mine. And it worked. George was happy. And he let Madison thrive in the company. That's the one good thing he did. He wanted his only heir to take over when he retired, and he made sure she had all the experience she needed to do just that.

"She got her confidence back," he said. "And eventually, some happiness." Scott turned away, looking out the window. "Brief," he said, barely above a whisper. "Brief moments of happiness." He looked at Ana again. "But we both know that there was always only one person for Madison. One person who lit up her world."

Ana lowered her gaze. "Thank you for telling me that." She found herself reliving the loss all over again. She'd never known such deep pain, and it was something she never wanted to experience again, which was why everyone in her life was kept at arm's length. Even if someone could have touched her the way Madison had, she wouldn't allow it. There was a slight sense of relief knowing she wasn't alone in that pain, but her heart felt so heavy. For both of them.

"Things were bound to change for us when George died," Scott continued. "Madison never said anything, but I figured she'd reach out to you, and what that means for us is yet to be determined."

Ana shook her head. "If you think Madison and I—" She paused for a moment. "What happened between us isn't something I can—"

"Forgive?"

Ana stared at him for a moment. "Forget. Those are two different things."

"Are they?"

Ana took a deep breath. She was starting to get frustrated. "What are you really asking me, Scott? Do I plan to steal your wife away? No, I don't. And if you're looking for a way out of your marriage now that George is dead, I'm not it."

Scott's gaze fell. "I'm not sure. I just know I had a strong feeling that I should come and talk to you. We both love her. We both want what's best for her. Don't we?"

Ana didn't feel as if she owed him an answer. "You're the one she married."

"Only because she couldn't have you. And now that George is dead, there's really nothing stopping her. So, my question to you is, do you want Madison?"

Ana didn't answer.

"I know the woman I married. She has never been whole, not for one day, and I've always known why. She faked it enough for the rest of the world, but I always knew. Things changed when her father died." Scott took a breath and looked away for a moment. "Now, she can't keep up the façade She has been absolutely miserable since the moment she saw you at the funeral. But she's also been the most genuine version of herself that I've ever known. And that, Ana, is because of you. So, it's a simple question, really. Do you want Madison?"

Did Ana want Madison? That wasn't a simple question; it was a loaded one. Ana wanted Madison's body again, yes. Desperately. The little taste she'd had in the hotel room wasn't enough. And admittedly, she'd imagined it, their first time together in fifteen years. Filling that raw ache wouldn't suck. Fucking Madison on every flat surface in her home would probably get her wet. Not probably. Definitely.

The part that *would* suck—opening her heart to Madison again.

Ana stood up. She walked to the door and opened it for him, leaving her non-answer open to interpretation.

Scott took the hint and stood. He offered his hand again. "Thank you for seeing me. I know you didn't have to."

Ana took his hand. "I wish you both the best."

❖

Madison was going over the final details for her annual charity event. "God, I wish I didn't have to do this. Surely people would understand that my father died recently."

Jocelyn knew Madison better than that. Her foundation meant everything to her. In fact, it seemed to Jocelyn that it was Madison's only true joy in life. "You'll have a full house. You'll bring in millions. But hey, it's not like those kids don't have enough scholarships to go around. And come on, do they really need someone to give them a chance?" Jocelyn winked.

"Very funny. And of course, you're right."

"As usual," Jocelyn quipped before mustering up a bit of extra courage. "Madison, we both know your father isn't the reason you've been out of sorts." She waited expectantly for a reply, wondering if she'd been too forward with that statement.

Madison took off her reading glasses and dropped her pen. "No, you're right. On both counts."

Jocelyn leaned forward, glad that Madison's desk was between them. "I have two things to say. Number one, I want a raise. I'm the executive assistant to the CEO now, and my salary doesn't reflect that. And number two, he's dead."

Jocelyn had made assumptions about Ana Perez, but she increasingly felt as if they were accurate ones. George Prescott was a homophobic prick who often made his feelings known about Jocelyn's sexuality in a not so subtle way: growling under his breath about the picture she proudly displayed on her desk of Jocelyn with her girlfriend at an event. He never spoke the words—he would just growl and grimace, then burst through his daughter's office door like a bull in a china closet.

As if on cue, Jocelyn's reminiscing was interrupted. "I just spoke to the estate lawyer!"

Jocelyn jumped at the loud exclamation, then spun around in her chair to find George's sister, Nora, standing there with her hands on her hips. She turned back to her boss for direction.

"It's okay, Joss."

Jocelyn stood and picked up her pile of folders. "Don't worry. We got this, okay?"

Madison gave her a tired smile. "Thank you. I couldn't do it without you. We'll talk about your first point later today, but the short answer is yes."

Jocelyn swept past Nora, flashing her a wide smile on her way out. The little interaction she'd had with George's sister wasn't pleasant. Nora was almost as bad as her brother when it came the way she spoke to employees, treating them as nothing but underlings. Having been charged with managing all of the paperwork, Jocelyn knew what Nora was there for. She disliked the old shrew and took extra pleasure in knowing only one of them would be walking out of Madison's office with more money that day. And it wouldn't be Nora.

Nora sat where Jocelyn had just been. "I just spoke to the estate lawyer," she repeated in a more reasonable tone.

Here we go. Madison sat back in her chair. "I'm aware."

"Do you really believe I deserve that pittance? I'm a Prescott as much as you are a Prescott! And they were *my* parents, Madison. *My* parents built this company, not yours."

Madison was also of the opinion that what George had left his sister was disgraceful. She just hadn't figured out what to do about it yet.

"And nothing for my son? He is also a Prescott! And no matter what George thought, my father *loved* his grandson."

"I'm sure he did, Nora. No one is disputing that."

Nora leaned forward and narrowed her eyes. "No stock. No real estate. No shares in this company. Am I supposed to be happy with a measly two million dollars because I'm a woman? Would you be happy with that much? Knowing there are *hundreds* of millions?"

"Nora."

"Don't." Nora stood up and smoothed her hair. "Don't make excuses, Madison. Not when you gave that maid and the gardener and that son of a drug addict driver of yours nearly as much as you gave me." She sauntered to the door, swaying her hips as she went, and then turned back around. "You'll pay for this. No one treats me with such disrespect. Not George, and certainly not you."

CHAPTER THIRTEEN

The diamond teardrop earrings seemed like the right choice. Madison checked her dress in the mirror one more time. Tonight, she had to shine, but she didn't feel shiny. She felt cold. The last few weeks had taken their toll on her. She'd spent every waking moment at the office, dealing with the board members, putting out fires, assuring everyone that she could run the company just as well as her father. She wondered if any of it was worth it.

The one thing that had kept her going since her father's cancer diagnosis was knowing she'd see Ana again, sooner rather than later. The weight of everything, the huge responsibilities that would be put squarely on her shoulders, had somehow seemed lighter with that knowledge.

She glanced at the large diamond on her left finger. She'd always imagined she'd wear a simple band, something Ana could've afforded when they were teenagers. She would've been happy with anything she gave her and worn it proudly.

She'd considered sending Ana an invitation to the charity gala tonight but thought better of it, considering how they'd left things. The last thing she needed tonight was some kind of a confrontation that would make her cry. Just *seeing* Ana would probably make her cry. She tossed a lipstick into her clutch bag and took a final look at herself in the mirror. It would have to do.

"Always the most beautiful woman in the room." Scott met her at the top of the stairs. Madison turned and let him zip up the last few inches on her burgundy, floor-length dress. She tried not to think about all of the times he'd done that for her when it should have been Ana.

Ana would have zipped the dress and kissed her neck. She would have whispered something sweet in her ear. No, something naughty. *I can't wait to take this off of you later. Or on second thought, maybe I'll leave it on.*

Madison smiled at the imaginary memory. Her smile faded when she remembered that the Ana who would've said those words was dead. And Madison had killed her.

❖

Stephen opened Madison's door. He leaned down and offered his hand. "Ma'am?"

Madison got out of the car. "Stand in front of me while I adjust this dress."

"Yes, ma'am." Stephen stood close but looked away. "Are you all right?"

Madison stopped her movements. Sometimes, she forgot how well Stephen knew her. "You noticed the dead silence, huh?"

"Yes, ma'am. It concerned me."

Normally, Madison would be fielding phone calls on the way to the gala, but she wanted none of that tonight. If they hadn't prepared well enough, it was too late to fix it. She was glad for the silence. It gave her time to think about things. Ana. It gave her time to think about Ana.

She couldn't give up. No matter how angry Ana was, Madison couldn't give up on her. She'd call her at work on Monday, or better yet, she'd call Carmen tomorrow and get Ana's private number.

"I'm fine," Madison said. "I'm going to the city apartment after, then take Scott wherever he wants to go." She caught Stephen's eye and smiled. "I'm fine, okay?"

Stephen smiled back. "Yes, ma'am."

He backed away, and Scott took his place. Madison looked over his shoulder, surprised to see her aunt Nora in the crowd. She didn't look happy, of course. Why was she even there? Madison had invited her, but she hadn't insisted that she attend the event. She took Scott's hand, ready to greet people and talk to the press when there was a scuffle right in front of her. Someone was pushing their way through the crowd. And then she saw the gun.

❖

"*Hmmfff.* Leave me alone." Ana rolled onto her stomach and grimaced at the bad taste in her mouth. Her bedroom smelled like day-old wine, and she couldn't figure out why Kris would be calling so late, or at all, since they'd officially broken up.

The distinct dinging started again. Ana wished Kris would heed the advice of those dishtowels and let the hell go.

After a brief silence, the phone rang again. "Oh, for fuck's sake!" Ana grabbed her phone and slid her thumb across it. "What!"

"Ana?"

Ana grabbed her head. Her own loud voice had made it pound even harder. "Oh God."

She'd been drinking at night ever since her conversation with Scott. Dealing with the truth obviously wasn't her strong suit. Maybe that was because no one had ever given her a chance to learn how.

"Ana, what's going on?"

"Nothing. Too much wine."

"Drink some water," Kris said. "You need to be alert for this."

Ana sat up and threw her legs off the bed. She grabbed her stomach and headed for the bathroom. "What's wrong?"

"Just drink some water. I know how you are when you have a hangover."

"Just tell me, Kris!" Ana lifted the lid and knelt down in front of the toilet. She dropped the phone on the floor and put it on speaker.

"...husband is here. He's distraught and causing a scene in the ER. Dave is trying to calm him down, but I thought you should know."

"What? Whose husband?" She grabbed her head. The pounding was getting worse.

"Madison's."

Ana stared at the phone, not sure she'd heard right. "Scott? Why is he there?"

"I don't know all the details. Something happened at a charity event. You need to get here, Ana. Madison is...she's barely alive."

Ana put a shaky hand over her mouth. *Barely alive.* She leaned over and vomited into the toilet.

❖

Ana sat in a waiting room full of people waiting for news on Madison. If it was possible to be underdressed in a hospital waiting room, this was Ana's moment. In a sea of shimmering gowns and starched tuxedos, Ana wore yoga pants and a hoodie. She'd worn her share of gowns, of course, but the experience still pinpointed just how far removed Ana was from Madison's life. Jocelyn was the only person she recognized.

A man in a dark suit sat next to her. He had two cups of coffee in his hands. "I'm Stephen, Madison's driver. You probably knew my Uncle Bernard." He offered a cup to Ana. "Coffee?"

His eyes were red and swollen. There was a hole in the knee of his trousers and blood on his shirt cuff. Madison's blood. Ana closed her eyes for a second as images flooded her mind. She imagined Stephen kneeling over Madison, trying to help her. She blinked back her tears and took the cup of coffee. "Thank you, Stephen." She took a sip of the warm liquid. "My mom told me about Bernard's passing. He was a good man." She smiled. "I still have a necklace he gave me for my birthday." Her smile faded. "Do you know what happened?" Stephen looked confused. "With Madison, I mean," Ana clarified.

"I was going back to the driver's side of the car when it happened. I didn't see anything." He shook his head in despair. "There was so much blood."

Ana noticed his shoes. The shiny black leather had smears of blood on it. She felt dizzy. Her vision blurred, and the room felt as if it was closing in on her. She needed to get out of that stuffy room before she fainted. She handed Stephen the cup and rushed out of the room. She found a wall to lean against and bent over, hoping the dizziness would subside.

"Ana!" Carmen rushed down the hall.

"Mom." Ana opened her arms. She held on to her mother, grateful for the support.

"What happened?" Carmen held on to Ana's shoulders. "You look pale."

"I'm fine." Ana wasn't fine, but she didn't want her mother fussing over her. "We're waiting for an update on Maddy."

Carmen closed her eyes and said a quick prayer in Spanish. "A shooting? I don't understand."

Scott came around the corner. His tux was covered in blood. "Ana. Thank God you're here." He pulled her into a hug. "They said I can see her. Do you want to come with me?"

"No." The word came out before Ana had time to think. She didn't mean for it to sound as harsh as it did. "She needs *you*, Scott."

It didn't feel right to be in the room when Madison woke up. Not after the way they'd left things in California. Ana would take it all back now if she could—all of the harsh words. She'd take back the kiss too. It was a selfish act that only created more pain for both of them. It needed to stop. She was not the first person Madison needed to see.

Scott lowered his voice. "I know her heart, and it beats for you, Ana. She needs both of us in that room."

"Go," Carmen said. "Put aside whatever is in your head and go. And tell her I'll make her favorite treat when she's better."

Scott didn't give Ana a choice. He took her by the arm and led her down the hall to the ICU. The doctor met them at the door and explained why the surgery had taken so long. The bullet had ripped through Madison's lower abdomen, causing major blood loss and damage to her kidney. She was alive, thanks to the paramedics who had been hired to cover the event. Scott and Ana listened intently, holding on to each other the entire time.

Ana stayed back while Scott stood by Madison's bed. He took her hand and tried to say her name, but all he could do was cry. Ana took a deep breath and wiped her tears away with the sleeve of her hoodie. She summoned up enough courage to step up to the other side of the bed.

Scott stopped crying long enough to look at her and whisper, "Thank you."

Ana leaned in close and caressed Madison's cheek. "It's me, Maddy. I'm here."

2003

"Come on, jump in!"

Ana was nervous. She'd swam in the Prescott pool a couple of times when she was younger, but then one day, her mother told her she wasn't allowed to anymore. She said Mr. Prescott didn't allow anyone but his own child in the pool. Now, she was standing at the edge of the pool being egged on by Madison.

"He's out of town. He'll never know."

Ana wasn't so sure about that. "What if someone tells him?"

"Who would tell him? The staff hates him, Ana. And they love you. Besides, it's midnight. No one is awake." She pointed over to the staff quarters. "Do you see any lights on?"

Ana slowly dropped her towel, revealing a red bikini. She didn't mean for it to be sexy, but the look on Maddy's face told her it was. She giggled. "Stop looking at me like that."

Madison's eyes wandered down Ana's body and back up again. "You're so...I'm speechless."

"You? Speechless? Give me a break." Ana realized it was the first time Maddy had ever seen her in a bikini. And being a late bloomer, she finally had boobs. She decided to tease Maddy a little bit by dipping one toe in the pool. "I can't! It's too cold!"

"Yes, you can! Get in here!"

Ana stood on the edge with her arms folded and shook her head. "Nuh-uh."

Maddy went to the steps and got out. She was also wearing a bikini. Ana watched intently as she walked toward her. She was so beautiful with her wet blond hair and freckled nose. Ana was sure she'd never love anyone the way she loved Maddy.

"What's wrong? Are you scared? You know how to swim, right?" Maddy stood there, dripping wet, with her hands on her hips.

Ana giggled. "Of course I can swim, dummy!"

"Well, then—" Maddy put her hand on Ana's hip and pulled her closer.

"You're wet and cold!" Ana tried to squirm away, but Maddy had a tight grip on her. She stopped fighting it and relaxed when she saw Maddy's eyes fall to her cleavage. She put her arms around Maddy's neck and let the moment be what it was.

"God, you're beautiful, Ana."

Ana knew in that moment, she was ready. She wanted to belong to Maddy in every way. "Since we're going steady now—"

Maddy peeled her eyes from Ana's chest. "Yeah?"

"Do I get to call you baby or honey or some other term of endearment?"

"I like baby."

Ana turned them so Maddy's back was to the pool. "Okay, baby." She pushed Maddy into the pool and laughed hysterically.

Maddy shot out of the water, pushing her hair off her face. "You're in so much trouble, Ana Perez!"

Maddy was quickly making her way to the stairs again, so Ana jumped in on her own, and when she came up, Maddy was right there. She wrapped her legs around her girlfriend's hips. "You love me, and you know it, Madison Prescott."

Maddy wrapped her arms around Ana and pulled her close. "Since I was eight years old, Ana Banana."

Ana's expression changed to something more serious. "You're mine, right?"

Maddy smiled and rested her forehead on Ana's. "I'm yours, baby. All yours."

Present Day

Madison could hear a voice, she just couldn't do anything about it. Someone was telling her to wake up. "Try to open your eyes," he said again. She tried, but she couldn't make those damned eyelids budge. Why was it so hard? And why couldn't she move? When she tried, it hurt like hell. Whoever was telling her to wake up could go jump in a lake. She was too tired.

A warm hand squeezed hers. Another stroked her face. "Maddy, it's time to wake up."

It felt nice, the hand on her face. Warm. Soft. Familiar. The voice was soothing.

"Come on, baby. You need to wake up."

Ana? Madison said the name in her head, but for some reason, her mouth wouldn't work. Was this one of those weird dreams where she couldn't run or scream or even move? A nightmare that was not really a nightmare because Ana called her "baby," so it couldn't be all that bad?

"My mom wants to make her famous empanadas for us. Remember how much you used to love those, Maddy? Apple was always your favorite. That was the one thing you refused to share with me, remember?"

Of course, I remember. But why does it hurt so bad when I try to move? I feel like someone's sitting on me. Is someone sitting on me?

"So, wake up now. Wake up and tell me if you want apple or cream cheese empanadas. Or both. You can have both, you know. My mom never could say no to you."

Madison tried so hard to open her eyes. She could feel the tender kisses on her forehead and cheeks. She wanted so badly to return those kisses, but she just couldn't open her eyes.

"Please, God. Help her wake up," Ana whispered by her ear.

I'm here! If Madison could've cried, she would have. Why couldn't she respond? Why couldn't she open her eyes and take Ana in her arms and tell her everything would be okay?

❖

It wasn't working. Ana looked at Scott. He was gripping the bed rail so tight his hands were turning white. He gave her a nod, encouraging her to continue. She sat on the edge of the bed and hovered over Madison. She ran her fingers over that face she loved so much. There were a few lines around her eyes that hadn't been there before. Her eyebrows were more sculpted, and the freckles on her nose that used to be so pronounced had faded some. But it was the same girl she used to love. The same lips she'd kissed so many times.

She cupped Madison's cheeks and rested their foreheads together. "Come on, baby. Open your eyes."

Madison grunted.

"That's right. You can do this. You're strong, remember? So strong. Now, open your eyes, Maddy. I'm here."

Madison grunted again, and this time, one eye fluttered open and then the other. Ana smiled at her and whispered, "Good job, baby." She kissed Madison's forehead and stepped back to make room for the doctor.

Ana stood in the corner with tears of relief running down her face. She watched the doctor and nurses check everything and change bandages. Madison seemed to be going in and out of consciousness as the sedation wore off. Scott walked up to her and hugged her so tightly, she lost her breath for a second. "Thank you," he said. "I thought we might lose her forever."

Ana slumped in his arms. She was so tired she wasn't even sure what day it was.

"Go home and get some sleep," Scott said. "I'll call if anything changes."

❖

Ana opened the door to her apartment and knew by the smell of coffee brewing that her mom was there. "Mom?"

Her mom came from the bedroom. "How is she?"

Ana threw her coat over a bar stool. "She's still critical, but she's awake."

"Oh, thank God."

"I just need to sleep, Mom. Let me sleep for a few hours, and then I'll tell you what I know." Ana made her way to the bedroom and then turned back around. "Mom?"

"Yes, my love?"

Tears filled Ana's eyes. "Will you hold me?"

Her mom got a look of worry on her face. "You haven't asked that of me since—"

"Since the last time I lost her. I know."

❖

It was late afternoon when Ana finally woke up. Her mom had a bagel and coffee waiting for her when she got out of the shower. She sat on a stool at the kitchen island and relayed in detail everything she knew about the shooting and Madison's condition. Then with a deep sigh, she said, "But there's something else I need to talk about."

Her mom nodded. "There's something heavy on your mind. I can tell."

Heavy didn't even begin to describe it. "Before Madison was shot, Scott came to my office. He told his side of the story—what he witnessed when Madison and I broke up. And I got the feeling that he was telling me I could have her back if I wanted her."

Her mom's eyes widened in surprise. "Ana Margareta Maria Perez! I don't care what he says. They're married, and that is that."

"It's a marriage of convenience, Mom. He's gay. It worked for both of them while George was alive, but now he's dead, and times have changed."

Her mom shook her head in confusion. "Maddy married a gay man?"

"George didn't know. He thought it was a real marriage that would give him an heir. And Scott says his parents would have disowned him if they knew he was gay, so he chose to marry his best friend."

"And now Scott wants out of the marriage?" Her mom sounded confused but hopeful.

"Maybe. He was vague. I really don't know if he wants to leave, but I'm pretty sure he doesn't want her to be alone."

"Or maybe he cares enough for Madison to give her what she's always wanted." Her mom pointed at Ana. "You."

Ana pushed away the bagel she'd barely touched. "If only I believed that."

"I understand," her mom said. "For the last fifteen years, I also thought the worst about Maddy. I thought she'd used you. Played some sort of sick game with your heart. But now, I know the truth." She reached across the kitchen island for Ana's hand. "I'm not telling you what to do. I'm just telling you that Madison had no choice. Had she asked for my advice at the time, I would have told her to do exactly what she did. George would've made good on his threats, and she knew it. Protecting you was always her first priority."

Ana stood up and pushed her stool away from the island. "The fact that neither of you sees what's wrong with that is pretty much the whole problem."

It took Ana two days before she could return to the hospital. She told herself it was work that kept her away, but the truth was, she was afraid to go back. It was one thing when Madison was unconscious, but now that she was awake, Ana wasn't sure she was ready to confront her feelings. She wasn't even sure what she felt anymore. It was as though love had sex with hate and made a baby named confusion.

Ana tried not to make any noise when she stepped into the room. She took it as a good sign that there was less equipment by the bed and not so many needles and wires attached to Madison's body. She no longer had a tube in her throat, so she'd be able to speak.

Ana took a few steps closer, and Madison opened her eyes. They stared at each other for a moment before Madison closed her eyes again. Ana wasn't sure if that meant she should stay or go.

"Apple," Madison whispered. Her voice sounded weak.

Ana sat down. "I'll text my mom. You'll have apple empanadas for breakfast tomorrow."

"You called me baby." Madison opened her eyes. They were wet with tears.

Ana reached for her hand, caressing it with her thumb. "Yeah," she whispered back.

Madison closed her eyes. Her body started to shake.

"Hey." Ana stood up and leaned over the bed. "Don't cry. You'll make me cry."

Madison tried to lift her hand to Ana's face, but she was too weak. Her arm flopped back on the bed. "Stay," she whispered.

"I'll stay for a while." Ana wiped the tears from Madison's cheeks. "If you promise to stop crying."

Madison nodded. "I promise. Just don't leave."

CHAPTER FOURTEEN

Ana left the hospital room and found the nearest chair. She doubled over and put her face in her hands. Madison still loved her and always had—she had no doubt now. It was almost too much to take, knowing the life they'd missed out on but for one person who refused to just let them be who they were.

They couldn't turn back time. They couldn't get back the life that had been so savagely ripped from them. God, how Ana hated George Prescott. The hatred she had for him made her stomach roil. Any regret she'd had for spitting on the man's grave was long gone. In fact, she wished she'd done it in front of everyone instead of waiting until all the guests were gone.

But it wasn't just George. Every time she thought she had her anger toward Madison in check, it would bubble up to the surface again. If she'd just been honest with Ana fifteen years ago, surely, they could've found a way to be together. Why didn't she go to Ana? Why didn't she fight for them with everything she had?

"May I join you?" Scott sat next to her. "I just spoke with the doctor. He's optimistic."

Scott didn't look so good. Not like the put together man Ana had met at her engagement party and then in her own office. His face was pale, and his eyes were bloodshot. "That's good." She patted his knee. "No offense, but you look at bit worse for wear."

"No offense taken." Scott leaned over and clasped his hands together. "It was such a relief when George died. It was as if all of the curtains and windows in the house had been flung open, letting in fresh air and sunshine. I was so excited about the possibilities. And then, this happened."

"What possibilities?"

Scott shot Ana a look of surprise. "Just feeling free to be who we are, I guess. Not worrying about whether or not George would approve."

Ana turned in her chair so she was facing him. "Things like taking a long vacation? Painting the living room purple? What, specifically, would be different if George were still alive?"

Scott scratched his beard. "For starters, I wouldn't have this on my face. George would've given me hell at dinner every Sunday. Told me I looked like a miscreant or something equally flattering."

"And Madison? What would she do differently?"

Scott furrowed his brow. "Don't you know?" He turned in his chair as well. "You, Ana. All she wanted was to see you again. It kept her going, thinking you'd be there at the end of the George Is Dead rainbow."

"And she just assumed I'd forgive her? What, just welcome her into my life after what she'd done?"

"Don't you want to?"

The question hung in the air. Ana blinked back more tears. "I want her to get better so she can live the life she always wanted. But I can't be a part of it." She stood and took a few steps toward the elevator, then turned back around. "Take good care of her." Scott stood and looked as if he was about to say something but Ana didn't give him the chance. She walked away and didn't look back.

❖

Two long days in LA left Ana feeling bone tired. The business meetings had dragged on forever, followed by lengthy dinners with her colleagues. She dragged herself back to her hotel room, dropped her work bags, and grabbed the ice bucket. She filled the bucket and bought a Diet Coke from the machine.

She got undressed and put on a bathrobe, then scanned the mini-bar. She poured bourbon and Coke over ice and relaxed in a chair, taking a few sips before she placed the call.

"Did you go to the hospital today? How is she doing?"

"Is that how you greet your mother?"

Ana sighed. "Sorry. It's been a long day."

"You sound tired."

"I'm way past tired."

"Well, we won't have the conversation where I tell you that you work too hard."

Ana chuckled. "I think we just did."

"You're calling about Madison? This is a good sign."

"A sign of what?"

It was her mom's turn to sigh. "Never mind. She took a turn for the worse last night, but she's stable again."

Ana sat up. "What happened?"

"Infection."

"But she's okay now?"

"I hope so," her mom said. "I had to come home and shower. I'll sleep the night here and go back in the morning."

"Who's with her? Mom, you can't just leave her."

"Her husband is with her."

"He's not her husband. Not really."

Her mom didn't respond.

"What, Mom? He's gay. They don't sleep together. It's a fake marriage. I told you that already."

"He's a very nice man. We've talked quite a bit. And he's here. You're not."

Ana set her drink down a little harder than she meant to. "What is that supposed to mean?"

"If you care so much, Ana, come back and take care of her. Madison loves you. She needs you. She'll heal quicker if you're here."

Ana knocked back the rest of her drink. She started to say something, then stopped. "I can't."

"Work is not more important than this."

"Mom, don't. It's not work." She took a deep breath. "I need you to be there for her, for me. I can't do it. It hurts too much. Can you understand that? Can you understand how it breaks my heart just being in the same room with her?"

"It doesn't have to, my love. You could let go of the past. You could forgive."

Ana's jaw flexed. "She destroyed me. You, of all people, should know that. You watched what it did to me. Why would you, my own mother, want me to expose myself to that again?"

Her mom didn't respond right away. After a moment, she said, "And yet, you want me to take care of her."

Ana tipped her empty glass, letting the last few drops hit her tongue. She set it down and put her face in her hand. "Don't make me explain it, Mom. I'm so tired."

"Sleep, my love. And don't worry, I will take care of the love of your life."

"She's not—" The line went dead. Ana set the phone on the table and clasped her hands together. Why didn't anyone understand that no one could just turn back time and erase the past?

❖

Ana ran full speed down the hall. She threw the door to Madison's room open and took in the scene. The text from her mom had been frantic, but the doctors weren't there. Her mom walked over to her. "Thank you for coming so quickly."

"What's wrong?" Ana took off her jacket and threw it on a chair. "Why is Maddy crying?"

"She's been upset all morning. The stress of everything. The pain. Wondering who wants her dead. It adds up."

"I thought she had taken a turn for the worse," Ana whispered. "You can't send a text like that when nothing's wrong."

"I just told you what was wrong. She can't heal if she's upset. And I'm…" Her mom lowered her voice. "I'm a poor substitute for you, Ana. I can't soothe her the way you could. And she's not buying my excuses for why you're not here. She thinks you don't want to be here."

Ana shook her head in disbelief. "You scared me to death."

Her mom patted her arm. "I'm going to get something to eat. I expect you to still be here when I get back."

"When are you coming back?"

Her mom shrugged. "When I feel like it."

Ana rolled her eyes. "Great."

She waited until her mom had left the room before she went over to the bed. Madison's eyes were closed. She was whimpering. Ana couldn't tell if she was crying or dreaming. She leaned over the bed and put her hand on Madison's cheek. It was wet with tears. "Maddy? Honey, look at me. I'm here."

Madison opened her eyes and blinked a few times. "Hey."

Ana sat on the edge of the bed. "Hey. Why so sad?"

Madison looked away. "Where have you been?"

"LA"

"You got back three days ago."

Ana cringed. Her mom wasn't supposed to report Ana's every move. "It's been a rough week at work."

Madison turned and looked at her again. Her eyes were still full of tears. "You don't have to stay."

"No?" Ana smiled. "Maybe I could just write you notes and have my mom deliver them."

Madison grinned. "Like that time I had my tonsils removed?"

"I think I actually started a note with, Dear Maddy, I'm so jealous of you right now."

"It was the unlimited ice cream, right?" Madison reached up and pushed a lock of hair from Ana's eyes. "I love your hair short like this. Have I told you that?"

"Different from before, huh?"

Madison gasped for air as her emotions overwhelmed her again. "Sorry. Every little thing makes me cry."

Ana cupped Madison's cheek and wiped a tear away. "I remember what cheered you up when you had your tonsils out."

"You do?"

"Uh-huh." Ana kicked her heels off and lay on what little bit of bed was available, careful not to crowd the patient too much. "Cartoons!" She found the remote for the television and clicked a few buttons. "Damnit, does this thing even work?"

"You're staying?"

"Does it look like I'm going anywhere?" Ana pushed a few more buttons. "Aha! *SpongeBob SquarePants*." She put the remote down and looked at Madison. "I haven't seen this episode, have you?"

Madison giggled. "No, but I have always wondered what a SpongeBob is."

Ana draped some of the blanket over her bare legs and rested her head on Madison's pillow. It felt just like old times, minus the gunshot wound and all of the lies. She decided to forget about that for the next half hour and watch SpongeBob irritate the hell out of Squidward.

"Wanna hold hands?"

Ana snickered. "Really, Maddy? You're going to ask to hold my hand right now?" She glanced at Madison. She was grinning. "Oh my God. Okay." She put her hand out, and Madison took it, interlocking their fingers. Ana shook her head and laughed under her breath. "You're something else, Madison Prescott."

"And you're everything, Ana Perez."

❖

Ana stirred awake. She lifted her head and tried to get her bearings. Madison was sleeping soundly next to her. That was good. Ana's mother was sitting in a chair, grinning from ear to ear. "How long have you been here?"

"Not long."

Ana looked at her watch. They'd been asleep for a few hours. "How long is not long?"

"Oh, maybe an hour." She glanced around, feigning innocence. "Or two."

Ana got up and slid into her heels. She leaned down and inspected Madison, wanting to make sure her breathing was steady. Madison opened her eyes and smiled. "Hey, Banana."

Ana grinned. "Hey, you. My mom is here."

Madison turned her head. "Hey, Carmen."

Ana lifted an eyebrow. "You get shot and you call her Carmen?"

Her mother stood. "Don't be silly, Ana. Madison and I go way back." She winked and took Madison's hand in hers. "How are you feeling?"

"Like I've been caught sleeping with your daughter."

Ana put her hands on her hips. "Oh, we're making jokes now?"

"Better than crying," Madison said. "Do you have to go?"

"I do. Work. Life."

"I understand. Thank you for watching *SpongeBob* with me."

Ana held back any words that would commit her to coming back. "Focus on getting better, okay?"

Madison gave her a nod. "Okay."

Ana left the room and ran into Scott coming down the hall. "Ana. It's good to see you." He held up one of the cups of coffee in his hands. "This is for your mom. She's been here every day with Madison. I can't thank her enough."

"Good," Ana said. She pointed down the hall with her thumb. "I have to run."

"Hey, Ana." Scott tilted his head. "I don't want to embarrass you, but I saw the two of you sleeping in there."

"Oh God." Ana covered her eyes. "It was nothing. I was just there to calm her down. She'd been crying."

"It's okay. I just wondered if we'd reached the point where we could talk about how much you still love her."

"Scott, I need to go." Ana didn't have time for a bullshit conversation. Did she still love Madison? On some level, yes. She'd dropped everything without a second thought and rushed to the hospital, hadn't she? That meant something. But the kind of love Scott was talking about was a different story. That kind of love required forgiveness. It meant putting everything aside and opening up one's heart and saying, it's yours again. Have at it.

Ana's heart was firmly locked behind a vault, and she planned on keeping it that way. "And no," she said. "We're definitely not to that point."

CHAPTER FIFTEEN

Six Months Earlier

Madison ushered her father's attorney out of her father's bedroom for the last time. "Is everything in order, Nigel? Any last-minute changes I should know about?"

Nigel put his hand on Madison's shoulder and spoke in a softened tone. "He wants to give a thousand dollars to your mother's church, in her name."

Madison rolled her eyes. "A thousand dollars won't put him right with God."

"No. I imagine it won't."

"I'm sure he spends that much on a day of golf with his buddies," Madison said under her breath.

Nigel gave her a sympathetic nod. "Maybe we could donate a new bench to the church for their garden. Have your mother's name engraved on it."

"I'd like that, Nigel. Thank you." Madison let out a heavy sigh. There was so much to consider. So much to do with the impending funeral. But another question still loomed large in her mind. "And he still refuses to leave anything to the staff?"

Nigel frowned. "I'm sorry, Madison. I wish I could change that."

They walked together to the stairs. "It's okay. You have to do your job, and I have to do mine. I'll find another way to compensate them."

"I'm sure you will."

"I appreciate your dedicated service to our family, and I'm sure I'll see you in a few days."

Nigel kissed Madison's cheek. "Let me know if I can help with the funeral arrangements."

"I will. Thank you." Madison waited until he was down the stairs before she went back to her father's room. She stood in the doorway, taking in the scene. The large, four-poster bed sat empty. George had been relegated to a hospital bed over a month ago, much to his chagrin. It sat in the middle of the room so the nurse could easily care for him from either side. George had fought it, of course, believing that the only person whose comfort mattered was his own. The damn nurse could crawl across the bed if needed. Typical George at his best.

His strong, tall form had withered away to almost nothing, but he still managed to insult everyone who had the misfortune of crossing paths with him. That much hadn't changed. Nothing would change the man, not even the knowledge that he was days away from meeting his maker. Of course, that's probably what the last-minute donation to the church was for. But George was assuming he'd see heaven. Madison wasn't so sure.

She sat on the edge of his bed and removed his oxygen mask. "There are some things we should talk about before you die, George."

He reached for his daughter's hand and squeezed it, fighting for every breath he took. "I keep thinking about your mother. I miss her."

Madison looked at the hand resting on her own. Should she comfort him, knowing he'd be gone soon? No. That wasn't why she'd walked back into this room. He had very little strength left, so she easily pulled her hand out from under his. "I miss her too. She was a good woman. How she ended up with you, I'll never know."

George tried to laugh but coughed instead. The long years of smoking cigars and cigarettes had finally caught up with him. He took in a few shallow breaths and said, "She married me for my money, that's how."

If only he were joking. If only he would use his last breath to say something good. Maybe admit his failures. His sins against his family. Anything! But this was George. And Madison knew better than to hope for something kindhearted. "You're wrong about that, Dad. You were always so wrong about her. You locked her up in this big house and broke her spirit, but you didn't break mine, hard as you tried."

"Everything I ever did was for your own good." George tried to reach for his oxygen mask, but Madison pulled it away. It was time for her to say her piece before he took his last breath.

"No, Dad. You never cared about me. Not really. You cared about your reputation and your standing in the community, but it's time you know the truth, and as your only child, I think it's my duty to tell you that everyone hates you, including me." Madison leaned in and lowered her voice. "I hate you with every fiber of my being. The staff hates you. Your friends call you the Prescott dinosaur— forever stuck in the dark ages. The board members can't wait for you to die so they can sell off your company one piece at a time. And one more thing. No, the most important thing of all is I still love a woman named Ana Perez. I'm still madly in love with her, and the second you stop breathing, I'm going to find her, and I'm going to apologize until I'm blue in the face. I'm going to apologize for both of us, Dad. Because what we did to her was beyond the pale. And honestly, I hope you rot in hell for it. Me, I'm going to pray I can make it up to her, but you have no fucking chance."

George attempted to lunge forward, trying to grab Madison's arm, but she quickly stood up. She watched him for a moment as he struggled for every breath, their matching blue eyes boring into each other. She remembered all of the kisses on the cheek he'd given her on special occasions, never telling her he loved her, only that he was "pleased" with her choices. As if they were ever really her own choices.

"I'm going to change the Prescott legacy, Dad. Your legacy dies with you. My legacy is the one people will remember and celebrate. It's my name, Madison Prescott, that will go down in history. George Prescott III will be but a small blip on a Wikipedia page, remembered only by those who are as small-minded as he was."

"What have you done, Madison? What have you been doing behind my back?" George gasped for air. Sweat started to bead on his forehead from the effort.

Madison's eyes narrowed, her lips curling into a smile. "Just rest, Dad. All that money will be put to good use. Remember Carmen Perez, the maid you kicked out onto the street in the middle of the night? The one who had been so loyal to you for years? She'll soon own stock in your beloved company. Lots of it."

Madison patiently watched and waited, out of harm's reach, for her father to try to get enough air into his lungs so he could speak again. It was obvious he had a lot to say. "What, Dad? What do you want to say?"

George managed to sit up enough to reach the oxygen mask and hold it to his mouth for a few seconds. "Get Nigel back here, now! Get my lawyer." It was only a few seconds before he flopped back down on the bed, holding the mask tightly to his mouth.

"I'll get the nurse. You're obviously in pain and need more morphine, but one more thing before I go." Madison leaned in close to his ear, keeping her hands behind her back so he couldn't grab her. "Scott and I lied. It wasn't that we couldn't have children; it was that we couldn't stand the thought of our child knowing their grandfather. But you'll be dead soon, so maybe Ana and I will go ahead and have that heir you so desperately wanted."

Madison waited because George never could let his daughter have the last word. He pulled the mask away. "That little bitch of yours—" He sucked in air for a few seconds. "Only got to where she is because she gives good head. She's been sucking—" He choked on his own words, coughing up blood.

Madison straightened up and glared at him. It never seemed to matter to George that his only child was a girl. He spoke to her exactly the way he'd speak to his son if he'd had one. "So little breath left and that's how you choose to use it? Making up lies about a person you never bothered to get to know? And besides, Dad, you've played that card before, you sorry son of a bitch. I didn't believe it the first time you said it, and I sure as hell don't believe it now." She leaned in close again. "I'm sure you thought you'd live a lot longer than this, and that you'd be able to control my every move until I was old and gray. But guess what, Dad? Karma's a bitch. And after I've buried your sorry ass, I'm going to donate a million dollars to charities that champion gay rights across the country. In *your* name. George Prescott III proudly donates, blah, blah, blah." Madison stepped back as George tried to grab her.

"Don't you dare ruin my good name," he muttered through the oxygen mask.

Madison scoffed at that. "I have news for you. Your name was never any good." She went to the door and then turned back around one more time. "Good-bye, Dad."

Present Day

"I know you've only been home for a few days. I appreciate you taking the time to see me."

Madison and Scott had been answering the detective's questions for over an hour. "I'm sorry I don't have more for you," she said.

"We'll get them, Mrs. Prescott. You just worry about getting better."

Scott let go of Madison's hand and stood. "I'll see you out."

Madison moved to the desk in her father's library. It was still his and would be until she could get a decorator in there.

She stared at the phone number Carmen had scribbled on a scrap of paper. Should she call Ana? Should she leave her alone? She hadn't seen her since that day in the hospital when they'd fallen asleep watching cartoons. Madison smiled at the memory. It felt heavenly being so close to Ana again. Holding her hand. Breathing her in. God, she wanted more of it.

She took a deep breath and put the phone to her ear because life was too damn short, she'd recently discovered. After several rings, Ana's voice mail message came on. Hearing her voice made Madison smile. "Hey, it's me. You probably didn't answer because you don't recognize the number. It's okay. We haven't spoken on the phone in a very long time, but you don't have my private number, so anyway, I'm rambling." Madison rolled her eyes at herself. "I just wanted to…" She started to tear up. "I just wanted to hear your voice, you know? We haven't really spoken since that day in the hospital. And I don't know if I'm allowed to say this, but I miss you. And I know we didn't exactly leave things in a good place in California. And just because I got shot doesn't wipe that away. I know that. But I miss you." She wiped her eyes and took another deep breath. "Okay. That's all I wanted to say. Bye, then."

She set the phone down and clasped her hands together. She didn't really understand why Ana was keeping her distance. Carmen had been there for her, accompanying her home from the hospital and helping her get settled in. She'd visited her several times since as well, but she never had a good answer as to why Ana hadn't kept in touch. They'd had a moment in the hospital. A good moment. Ana had let Madison hold her hand. It felt good. It felt right. Just like it always had.

2003

"Tell me this gorgeous body belongs to me," Madison whispered.

They'd been swimming and lying out in the sun for hours, so Ana was sure she'd have tan lines. They were in Madison's bedroom, which always made her a little nervous, even if George was out of town. Ana didn't trust the staff the way Madison did. She and her mother got along really well with all of them, but it was still risky.

"Of course, it does," Ana whispered back. "But—"

"But what?" Madison kissed Ana's ear.

Ana giggled. "You're giving me goose bumps."

"You're not ready for more?"

Ana was very ready for more. Her body felt crazy things whenever she was close to Madison. And when they kissed— she couldn't even begin to describe what Madison's kisses did to her. She just needed to feel safe, so she walked over to the door and locked it. Then she turned around and untied her bikini top, holding it in place with her other hand. She wasn't sure where this courage was coming from, but she tried to ignore how hard her hands were shaking.

Madison was also wearing her bikini top with her cut-off jean shorts. She mimicked Ana's actions, untying her top as well. Ana suddenly felt afraid, not knowing what their next move should be.

"Come here," Madison said, holding out her free hand.

Ana walked over to her. "I'm not sure…" She looked at the floor. "I've never…have you?"

"No," Madison admitted. She put her finger under Ana's chin and looked her in the eye. "I've been waiting for you." She took Ana's hand and led her to the bed. "We don't have to."

"I want to," Ana whispered, her eyes locked on Madison's chest now.

Madison reached back and untied her own bikini top completely, letting it fall away to their feet. Ana's eyes widened at the sight. Madison's breasts were so pale and perfect. "Oh God," she whispered, taking in shallow breaths. She summoned up the courage to untie her own top and as it fell away, she reached for Madison's hips and pulled her closer so their breasts touched.

They stood that way for a moment, lost in the feel of bare skin on bare skin. "Are you okay?"

Ana pulled back slightly so she could look at Madison's body again. She ran her finger from Madison's bellybutton up to just barely between her breasts, her touch soft and tentative. "You're sunburned."

"I know. I wish I was like you. You never burn. Plus, you look like a Mayan goddess."

Ana giggled. "A what?"

"You know," Madison said. "A Mayan—"

Ana cut Madison off with a kiss, her hands gripping at her waist. She felt that feeling again, that crazy beating in her chest and the butterflies in her stomach and the heat building throughout her body. She'd never been brave enough to do it before, but it felt right now, so she let her hands drop to Madison's hips and then to her ass. She heard Madison moan, and she took that as a good sign and pressed their bodies together, her hands pressing into the tight flesh.

Madison pulled away from the kiss first, trying to catch her breath. Her eyes grazed Ana's naked chest. "God, you're so beautiful, Ana. Can I touch you?"

"You don't have to ask. I'm yours, remember?"

With a feather-light touch, Madison brushed Ana's long brown hair off her shoulders. She ran her fingers over taut nipples. "I can't believe I'm doing this," she whispered, her eyes alive with wonder. She leaned in and kissed Ana's shoulder, then her neck. With the back of her fingers, she caressed Ana's stomach and slowly worked her way up to her breast. "You feel so good."

Ana wanted to faint. She felt dizzy. Madison's soft voice, her sweet kisses, her hands—it was almost too much. "So do you."

Madison ran her hand back down Ana's side and around to her ass. She slid her hand into her bikini bottoms. Ana gasped. Madison stilled her hand. "Is this okay?"

Ana pushed Madison away. Her chest heaved. She just needed to catch her breath, but seeing the girl she loved standing there half-naked made her not care anymore. She didn't care if this was right or wrong. She didn't care about anything except Madison.

Ana lunged back into her arms and kissed her as if they'd never kissed before. It had always been soft and gentle when they'd kissed. This was something different. And Ana decided that having Madison's tongue dance with her own was quite possibly the best feeling in the world. It made her insides tingle. It made her heart soar. It made her feel things she'd never felt before. Big things. And she wanted more.

It was Ana who pushed them onto the bed. It was Ana who slid Madison's shorts off of her body. They kept their bikini bottoms on while they kissed and touched each other. The room spun when Madison's warm lips touched Ana's breast for the first time. And it kept spinning when her hand slid into the front of Ana's bikini bottom.

It was amazing how good it felt, but Ana didn't have words. She wanted to tell Madison how much she loved her. She wanted to say everything all at once. But the spot Madison was touching was causing her hips to have a mind of their own, and her brain had shut down or something because she couldn't think straight. And then, all at once, it felt as if the world literally exploded. And Ana screamed. And Madison put her hand over Ana's mouth and giggled. And then, Ana could say it. She could say the words, "I love you, Maddy. I will always love you and only you."

Present Day

Madison had just turned off her light and settled into bed when her phone rang. She smiled when she saw the number. "Ana."

"Hi." Just that one word gave Madison a small measure of relief. "I hope it's okay that I called. How are you doing? You know, with the injury?"

"Let's call it what it is," Madison said. "Someone tried to kill me, and my injury is a gunshot wound."

"Do you still think your aunt Nora had something to do with it?"

"I don't have any proof. I'm hoping the police will find it."

"It's hard to believe," Ana said.

"Well, somehow she found out that I'd given certain members of the staff some shares in the company. I planned on doing something for her as well. I just hadn't figured out what yet. I wasn't sure what would make her happier: for me to give her son a position in the company or just throw money at them. I was trying to figure out a respectful way to handle it, and then this happened."

"Well, if she's responsible, I hope they figure it out."

Madison chuckled. "And if she's not, I guess I owe her an apology. I just can't imagine who else, besides you, would want me dead."

"Don't say that. Don't ever say that, Maddy. I never wanted you dead. George, maybe, but never you."

"Promise?" Madison could feel the tears threatening again.

"I promise."

As long as she had Ana on the phone, Madison didn't want to leave anything unsaid. She'd say it all and hope for the best. If Ana couldn't accept her words, it would be okay. At least she wouldn't add to her long list of regrets by not saying anything. "Ana."

"Yes?"

"I loved you, Ana. I loved you so much, I wanted to run away with you and get married. Leave everything behind and just be us."

"I know," Ana whispered.

"Do you? Do you really know?"

It took a moment for Ana to answer. Madison was just about to look at her phone to see if the call had dropped when Ana said, "I was thinking about us when you called. Remembering stuff I'd pushed from my mind."

Madison sat up. "What stuff?"

"Bikinis."

"Ana."

"Don't, Maddy."

"Our first time?"

"Maddy."

"You brought it up." Madison knew what was coming. "Don't hang up, Ana. It'll kill me if you hang up. I feel like I'm losing everything all over again."

"Me too," Ana whispered. "And I can't go through it again."

"We don't have to. Ana, please."

"We can't undo everything George did to us. The scars will always be there. The pain…will always be there."

Madison heard Ana's sniffles through the phone. She'd said what she wanted to say. If she pushed it, she'd only cause Ana more pain. She set aside her own desires and said, "Could you promise me one thing? Don't forget the good stuff. Remember us when we were happy. Remember your apartment at Princeton. All the times we—" *Made love.* Madison squeezed her eyes shut, trying to fight her own tears.

"I'll try," Ana said. "Bye, Maddy."

❖

Ana had been staring at her phone for going on ten minutes. She wanted to call Madison when she'd heard the news. Just hear her voice, even if it was only for a few seconds. The problem was, those few seconds would cause days of suffering due to thinking about everything that was taken from them. A casual friendship couldn't make up for that. It only made it worse.

The good news was, Nora's son and the man he'd hired to do the killing were in police custody. According to Carmen, Nora was still claiming her innocence, saying that she'd made the mistake of complaining to her son about the inheritance but that his actions were his own.

Ana jumped when her phone rang, almost falling off the barstool in her kitchen. She righted herself and answered it. "Hi."

"Hey," Kris said. "You answered." Ana didn't reply. "Anyway, I just wanted to see how you were doing. We haven't talked since the hospital. Since the shooting."

"I'm okay," Ana said. "Just working too hard, as usual."

"Yeah, me too. Wanna go for a ride?"

"A ride?"

"Your baby," Kris said. "Let's take her for a ride."

Ana hadn't been on her horse in over a month. Not since Madison's accident. It was definitely time to get back in the saddle. "Are you saying you want to still be friends with me, Kris? Because you know I can't—"

"Friends, Ana. We were friends before we were ever lovers, and I miss that. So, what do you say to a day with me and Queen Isabelle?"

Ana smiled. "Her name is Isadora."

Kris chuckled. "Right. Isadora. The most spoiled horse I've ever met."

Ana sighed. "Okay. You're right. I need to get out of the city. I'll pick you up at 8:30."

"We can do this, Ana. We can be friends. I promise."

"Good. I could use one of those. And Kris? Thank you."

CHAPTER SIXTEEN

Ana took the corner a little faster than she should have. "Are we in a hurry?" Kris gripped the seat, her fingernails digging into the black leather.

"Relax," Ana said. "I know these roads like the back of my hand. I grew up here, remember?"

They were on the road that led to Madison's estate. They'd drive right past it in a minute. There were two ways to the stables, but Kris didn't know that. Madison's road was the shortcut, and over the years, Ana would choose one or the other depending on her mood. If she was in a dark mood, she'd take Madison's road and speed past the estate in her expensive car. She was no longer an interloper in this part of the world. She belonged here, if success and wealth were the measuring stick.

Ana took another corner at breakneck speed. "Hey, are you hungry? Do you mind if we stop at my favorite diner and have breakfast before we ride?"

Kris' eyes lit up. "You know me. I'm always hungry."

❖

Scott walked up behind Madison. "Everything okay?"

Madison stared out the window. "Stir crazy."

"Let's go for a walk around the grounds. It's a beautiful day."

"I'd rather go into town," Madison said. "Maybe pick up some fresh croissants from the bakery."

"Are you sure you're up for that?"

Madison hadn't been off the property, except for doctor's appointments. She was sick of all the silence. She wanted to be around people again. She wanted her daily rides into the city with Stephen. She wanted the chaos of work and that sense of accomplishment she often felt at the end of a long day. But that couldn't happen until the doctors gave their approval for her to return to work. *Stay calm and heal,* those were their words.

She was sick of it. "Let's take the convertible." She turned around, and with a look, dared Scott to argue with her.

He put up his hands and backed away. "Okay."

Ana pulled into the parking lot and noticed the silver vintage Mercedes convertible parked in front of the bakery that shared the building with her favorite diner. It looked just like the one George Prescott used to drive on the weekends while wearing his fedora and smoking a big, fat cigar. "They have great bread," she said, pointing at the bakery. "I know how much you love good bread."

"Yum," Kris said. "Can we go in there first? I'd hate for them to run out of croissants."

Ana turned off the engine and got out. She was just rounding the front of the car when she stopped dead in her tracks. "Maddy."

"Ana."

Kris stood next to Ana. "We were never formally introduced." She put out her hand. "I'm Kris."

Madison took her hand. "Yes, hello again. Madison Prescott."

It was awkward for Ana. She didn't want to bring up the engagement party where they'd all seen each other. "Kris, this is Scott Fairmont, Madison's husband."

"Yes. We met at the hospital. Good to see you under better circumstances, Scott."

"You too," Scott said. He leaned in and kissed Ana's cheek, then held up a bag. "We were just getting some chocolate croissants for breakfast."

"I hope you didn't buy the last one," Kris said. "They're my favorite."

Madison shook her head. "No. They have a few left."

Ana couldn't take her eyes off of Madison. She had on tight jeans with a long black sweater and tall black boots. Her blond hair was pulled back into a low ponytail. She looked incredible. "You look good," she finally said. "How are you feeling?"

Madison shrugged. "Looks can be deceiving." She tilted her head. "Are you going riding?"

Ana glanced down. She'd forgotten she was wearing her riding pants. "Yeah." She pointed down the road. "The stables where I board my horse are about five miles that way. We were hungry, so we stopped for breakfast."

"And croissants," Kris added.

"We should let them get to it." Scott looked at Madison, but she didn't move.

"I want to see your horse," Madison said, her eyes locked on Ana.

"I don't know if that's a good idea," Scott said. "You know what the doctors said."

"I didn't say I was going to ride it."

"We still need to have breakfast," Kris said.

"I have time." Madison gave Kris a smile.

"This is your first time getting out of the house, Maddy. Don't overdo it." Scott took Madison's elbow.

Kris wrapped her fingers around Ana's arm. "Let's go get those croissants."

"Her name is Isadora," Ana blurted out, stopping everyone. "She's a beauty. We'll get a muffin and eat it in the car. Follow us?"

Kris's shoulders slumped. Scott sighed. And Madison—well, Madison's eyes lit up. "Yeah. We'll follow you."

❖

"How are you *really* doing?" Ana had her arms folded as they walked to the stables. Kris and Scott were deep in their own conversation several feet behind them.

Madison glanced at her and smiled. "Honestly, I'm going stir crazy, and Scott's constant hovering isn't helping. I can't move without him questioning why I'm moving. But your mom visits me two or three times a week, and that means the world to me."

Ana leaned in, "Good. She needs someone else to worry about besides me."

"Well, trust me when I say she still worries about you," Madison said. Ana started to reply but stopped. Madison looked at her. "Please, don't censor yourself."

"I was just going to say that I really am sorry for what you've been going through. It's been a lot, with your father dying and trying to fill his shoes at work and then the shooting."

Madison let out a little laugh and shook her head.

"What?" Ana gave her a nudge with her elbow. "Don't censor yourself, either."

Madison sighed. "You're right. It's been a difficult time. But the physical pain is nothing compared to the pain of losing you."

Ana wrapped her arms a little tighter around herself. She was so used to believing that she was the only one who had felt the loss fifteen years ago that every time she heard Madison say it, it almost felt like a punch to the gut. "I didn't know," she whispered. "I believed you, Maddy, when you said you didn't want me anymore."

"I know. I needed you to believe me." She put her hand on Ana's arm and stopped. "I knew you'd fight for me to your death. Literally, to your death. And I couldn't let that happen."

Ana nodded and started walking again. She took a deep breath and then glanced at Madison and smiled. "As long as we're being honest, you look beautiful today."

Madison met her smile. "You should see my scars."

"Scars make us who we are, for better or for worse. This is her," Ana said, pointing to one of the stalls. Speaking in a soft voice, she said, "Hey, girl. Sorry I haven't been around much." She took Madison's hand and pulled her closer. "Isadora, this is Maddy." Isadora whinnied as if on cue. "Yes, Isadora. She's *that* Maddy—the one you've heard so much about."

"She's gorgeous." Madison stroked Isadora's neck and turned to Ana again. "Just like her owner in her cute riding pants."

Ana grinned. "Yeah, I always loved it when you'd show up in your jodhpurs and those boots and that fabulous jacket. God, you were sex—" Ana's smiled faded when she saw Scott standing there. She grabbed a brush and offered it to Madison. "Wanna help groom her?"

"She shouldn't," Scott said. "She's not supposed to exert herself. Stay calm and heal, remember?"

"You should listen to your doctor." Kris took the brush from Ana's hand. "So few people do."

Ana looked away so she wouldn't embarrass herself by saying the wrong thing out loud. She was happy that Scott was taking good care of Madison. But she also wanted to punch him in the face. It was an irrational feeling, considering she didn't have, nor did she want, any claim to Madison. She took a deep breath and smiled. "Right. Well, it was good to see you both."

"We'll have you over for dinner sometime," Madison said. "Maybe Thanksgiving?"

"Of course!" Scott said. "We're having my family over for Thanksgiving, but there's always room for more."

"Oh." The last thing Ana wanted to do was commit to an awkward few hours with strangers. "That's very nice of you, but

I don't think—" Ana noticed Madison's eyes were closing. She grabbed her elbow. "Are you okay?"

"Just a little dizzy is all." Madison put her hand against her forehead. "I guess we should go." She took Scott's arm and turned to leave.

Ana grabbed Madison's hand, the one that wasn't holding on to Scott. Their eyes locked for a second, and then in a bold move, she took Madison into her arms and held her close. "I'm so glad you're going to be okay," she whispered. Before Madison could get her arms around Ana and return the hug, Ana let go and backed away. "Take care," she added, and then turned and walked toward the tack room.

❖

"Did you have fun?"

Ana pulled into the hospital parking lot. "I needed that so much. Isadora needed it too." She put the car in park and turned to Kris. "Thank you for forcing me to take a break."

"No one forces Ana Perez to do anything. I just gave you a nudge."

"Are you saying I'm stubborn?"

"As the day is long," Kris said. "But that never deterred me. It just made me work a little harder is all."

Ana's smile faded. "I'm sorry about the engagement party. I know that was awkward for everyone. Your parents, especially."

"But you're not sorry that we're not still engaged." Kris put up her hand when Ana started to protest. "No, let me say this." She took Ana's hand in hers. "You need to figure it out. This thing with Madison—just figure it out. Because we both know she's the only woman you've ever really loved." She leaned in and kissed Ana's cheek. "Call me soon. We'll do lunch."

CHAPTER SEVENTEEN

Ana was staring at her phone again. Kris's words had been ringing in her ears. *Figure it out. Just figure it out.* She should just do it. Just send a text and say whatever was in her heart. Good or bad, just lay it out there. She picked up her phone.

Hey, baby. I miss you. She groaned at herself and quickly erased the words.

Hey, it's me. Thinking about you. Every second of every day. She erased that one too.

Hey, it's me. Say something that's true. Something I can believe in. That's the one she sent. Of all the texts in all the world. That's the text she sent. She felt like an idiot the second she hit send. She felt like an even bigger idiot when her phone almost instantly signaled a reply.

Are you okay?

Ana looked at the text and laughed. "No, Maddy. I'm not fucking okay," she responded out loud to exactly no one. She cringed as she typed in her response. *Yeah. Too much wine. Sorry.*

Her phone rang. "Shit." She stared at Madison's number. Should she answer it? She took a quick sip of wine. Because that had served her well so far. "Hey."

"Hey. Starting the holiday early?"

"Holiday?" Ana looked at the date on her watch. "Oh, yeah. It's Thanksgiving tomorrow. I forgot."

"Are you spending it with someone?" Madison's voice sounded hesitant, as if she was afraid to hear the answer to her question.

"Oh, I'm sure my mom will come over and force me to eat turkey."

"You hate turkey."

Ana laughed. "You remember that, huh?"

"Vividly. You always wanted enchiladas on Thanksgiving."

"Who doesn't?" Ana grabbed a tissue. "It's good to hear your voice." She blinked back a few tears.

"Yours too," Madison said.

"I'm sorry I sent that text. I'm just a little…"

"A little what? Talk to me, Ana."

"A little sad, I guess." Ana covered her eyes with her hand. She shouldn't be doing this. She shouldn't be calling Madison and baring her soul. What was she thinking? "I should go."

"No! Don't go, Ana. I've been hoping you'd call. I wasn't sure if I should call you since, you know, you're back together with Kris."

Ana opened her eyes. "Who told you that?"

"No one. I guess I just assumed since you were together that day at the stables."

"No." Ana shook her head. "No, we're not. In fact, we're over for good."

"Oh. Is that why you're sad? Did you just break up?"

"God, no. Maddy, we're friends. Just friends."

"Oh. Then tell me, why are you sad?"

Ana took another sip of wine. "Oh, you know, things got real shitty about fifteen years ago. I lost the love of my life. And now that I've found her again, I can't even be friends with her."

"Why not?"

"Because." Ana blinked back more tears. "Being just friends isn't really in the cards for us, is it?"

Madison sighed deeply. "Ana."

"You know it's true, Maddy. Otherwise, you wouldn't have been worried about contacting me when you thought Kris and I were together."

"I just wanted you two to have a chance. I didn't want..." Madison stopped. "Okay, you're right."

Ana grabbed her stomach. "So, I've lost you again. As if the first time wasn't painful enough?"

"Where are you?"

"What?"

"Where are you, Ana? I'll come to you."

"No."

"Ana, I will not let you be alone right now. Are you home?"

Ana wiped her eyes and straightened her shoulders. "Don't come here."

"I'm getting my coat. I'll be there soon."

Ana stood up. "No!"

"I'm calling your mom."

Ana grabbed another tissue. "No. Slow down. Just, please, slow down, Maddy. Just stay on the phone with me, okay? I'll be sober soon and totally humiliated. Just talk to me until then, okay? I can't even think about you being on the road this late, and my mom is already in bed. You'll wake her for nothing if you call."

"Okay. But if you hang up on me, I'm calling your mother."

"I won't. I promise. How are you? Getting stronger?"

"A little bit better every day," Madison said. "I go into the city three times a week. I've wanted to call you so many times. Maybe go to lunch together."

"That would be nice. And torture."

Madison chuckled. "I know. God, I know. Seeing you at the stables was hard."

Ana let that sink in for a few seconds. "I cried after you left. God, I'm a fucking disaster right now."

"Don't hang up, Ana."

"I won't. I promised I wouldn't. And I keep my promises." Ana slapped her forehead. "Oh God, don't listen to me. I'm such an asshole."

"Do you remember what you said to me in the hospital? You said, 'I'm here.' And I'm saying that to you, now. I'm here, Ana. I'm not going anywhere. I'm here."

Ana gasped for air in between sobs. "Maddy."

"That's right. I'm here. And I love you. I always have."

Ana smiled through her tears. "I love you too," she whispered.

"And now that we've said it, we can say anything. Anything at all. No more holding back, okay?"

"Okay." Ana wiped her tears away and took another deep breath. "Then tell me, Maddy, would you really leave Scott for me? I'm not asking you to. I just want to know."

Madison didn't hesitate. "I've only ever done what I thought was best for you, Ana. I asked you to marry me because I thought we'd be so happy together. I thought I could make you happy. And then I left you because I wanted your life to be good. I wanted you to be safe and get everything you deserve in this life. I didn't want my dad fucking everything up for you and your mom. And it kills me to know that you never found the happiness I so wanted for you. I prayed for you to find someone who could fill the hole I left in your heart. I prayed for you to have those four kids you wanted with someone you loved. I did that, never really caring about my own happiness. And if I thought it would be best for you to be with me again...yes, I would leave Scott for you."

Ana needed time to absorb that. She was definitely drunk, and that answer was too long for her to immediately take in and comprehend. "Yeah," she said, breathing into the phone. "Heavy."

"Are you still drinking?"

"No. The bottle's empty."

"Good. Will you do something for me? Will you go get a glass of water and climb into bed?"

Ana rubbed one eye with the palm of her hand. She felt tired, and bed sounded good. "Yeah, I can do that."

Once she was settled in bed with earbuds in her ears, she closed her eyes. "Okay, I'm in bed."

"I've only ever had three close friends. One was you, of course. Another is Scott." Madison paused for a moment then said, "I want to tell you about the third one. He's my driver, Stephen."

"I met him at the hospital. He gave me coffee."

"He's a good man but totally misunderstood."

"How so?"

"Well, he was a cute kid, but he didn't know how to talk to girls. He didn't know how to talk to anyone, really. You see, his mother was a drug addict, so he'd basically raised himself."

Ana yawned. "That's terrible."

"I know. Anyway, I found out that one of the gardener's daughters thought he was super cute, but Stephen was too shy to talk to her. In fact, he refused to even look her way. So, one day, I sat him down and told him that his past didn't matter. Who his mother was didn't matter. The only thing that mattered was who he was. And I told him that I once knew this girl."

There was a pause. Ana opened her eyes.

"I once knew this girl."

Another pause. Ana could hear Madison sniffling.

"Every Christmas," Madison said. "I put up a stocking for that girl. And I put her engagement ring in it. That girl has never stopped being what I live for. And she's never been far from my mind or my heart.

"Stephen saw us together at the cemetery, and because he'd had the courage to ask about the woman who made me cry, I told him our story again. I told him that the girl he'd heard about years ago was real. She was flesh and blood and the love of my life. And she still is."

"Don't say that."

"I thought we could say anything now. Whatever is in our hearts."

Ana didn't reply. She worried that she'd never be able to get past her own anger or ever bring herself to trust Madison again. She feared that no matter how much she loved her, she wouldn't be a good partner to her. She was broken inside.

"It's okay," Madison said. "You don't have to say it back. I'm not sure I would be the best thing for you anyway."

That surprised Ana. "What are you talking about?"

"I've been thinking about my father a lot lately. He swore to his death that he wanted what was best for me. And I think he genuinely believed he was acting in my best interest."

Ana sunk a little deeper into her pillow and closed her eyes. "Then he had a fucked-up idea of what your best interest is."

Madison laughed. "Isn't that the truth? Even so, he stopped at nothing to make sure I had a certain life. The husband, the career, all the goddamned lessons—piano, tennis, skeet shooting. Because God knows that has come in handy." Ana's breathing slowed, and Madison paused. "You still with me?"

"Yeah, I'm still here."

"Good. Because the thing is, I realized how my father took control of every aspect of my life. He made every decision for me. He did awful things—supposedly, all for me. I never had a say in any of it. And I hated him for it. I doubt I'll ever forgive him." Madison took a deep breath. "Ana?"

"Yeah?"

"That's what I did to you. I finally understand why you can't forgive me. And I think you deserve a fresh start with someone who didn't put scars on your heart. Someone you trust. But you can't compare that someone to me. It isn't fair to them. Start over. Start believing in love again and the goodness in people. I want you to be happy. That's all I've ever wanted."

"Yeah," Ana said. "I'll get right on that." She yawned. "I'm so tired."

"Remember when you first got your cell phone, and I'd talk to you until you fell asleep? Let me do that again," Madison said. "Let me tell you how proud I am of you and the incredible career you've had. I'm so proud of you, Ana Perez. So proud."

CHAPTER EIGHTEEN

"Mom, you don't have to cook. Do you know how many restaurants in this city make Thanksgiving dinner?" Ana sighed into her phone, already well aware this was a losing battle.

"Don't be silly. We're Americans. And that means we make Thanksgiving dinner, just like all the other families in this country. And it means you pretend to like turkey, just like everyone else in this country."

"But you'll make way too much food that will just sit in my fridge and go bad. And then you'll have to come over and throw it all out. And then I'll feel guilty for being so wasteful."

"Stop arguing with me. I'm almost finished shopping, so put on your happy face and meet me in the lobby in fifteen minutes. I don't want to carry all the bags up by myself."

"I have a doorman and an elevator. I'll think you'll be just fine. Love you."

Ana felt like shit warmed over. Putting on her happy face was the last thing she wanted to do. She had one hell of a hangover, but she didn't want to tell her mom that. She'd just worry. So, she stuffed her feet into her Ugg boots and grabbed her keys. She'd be there when the taxi drove up, even if she had let her mom think her only daughter would leave her to bring up the bags by herself.

When she opened the door to her building, the cold New York air felt good against her skin. She loved this city. She loved that she'd made good in this city. She was wealthy compared to most people. Not compared to Madison, of course, but hardly anyone had that kind of money.

Her mom had been safe and secure in her situation long before Madison had given her stock in the company. Ana had made sure of it. Being kicked out of their home was something she swore to her mom she'd make up for. Ana was proud of herself. And last night, she'd found out that Madison was proud of her too. She was dozing off, but she'd heard the words: *I'm so proud of you, Ana Perez.*

But Madison didn't know the whole truth. "I'm a workaholic, Maddy. A fucking workaholic."

"Excuse me?"

Ana didn't realize the doorman had stepped outside. "Nothing, Tommy. Just talking to myself."

"Just let me know if you need anything."

Ana dug in her jeans pocket and pulled out a wad of cash. She didn't even bother to count it. "Here," she said as she stuffed it into his hand. "I don't say thank you enough, Tommy. But I really do appreciate what you do. Happy Thanksgiving."

Tommy looked at the wad of cash. There were at least three one-hundred-dollar bills, along with some twenties. "Thank you, Ms. Perez. I appreciate that. Can I help you with anything out here?"

"In a minute. My mom's coming with groceries for the holiday."

He clapped his gloved hands together. "Wonderful! I hope she's making empanadas. She makes delicious empanadas."

"I wish. She does a traditional American Thanksgiving." Ana smiled. "She worked her ass off to give me a good life. And now, she insists on making me a Thanksgiving dinner I probably won't even eat."

"Oh," Tommy said, shaking his head. "You should eat it. At least a little bit."

Ana laughed. "You're right, I should. Where's your family today?"

"Brooklyn, ma'am. All twenty-seven of them."

"Wow!" Ana said. "Big family."

"Family is everything."

Ana pointed at the cab. "Here's my family." Her mom got out of the car, and Ana didn't have to plaster a smile on her face. It was very real. "Hey, Mom."

❖

"Is it work?" Ana's mom took a bite of turkey.

Ana looked up from the plate of food she'd hardly touched. "What?"

"You're a million miles away."

"Sorry, Mom." Ana stopped stabbing at her food and took a big bite so as not to offend her mom. "It's delicious, as always."

"You're right. It is. But you're preoccupied, and I want to know why."

Ana could pretend it was nothing, but eventually, her mom would get it out of her, so she told the truth. "It's Maddy."

Her mom set her fork down. "Have you talked to her?"

"Yeah. Last night."

"And?"

"Actually…" Ana shook her head, trying to get rid of all the thoughts running through it. "Can we just eat?" She took another huge bite of mashed potatoes and smiled.

Her mom took a sip of wine and sat back in her chair. She studied Ana for a moment. "There's absolutely nothing stopping you from taking what is rightfully yours."

Ana stopped mid-bite. "Huh?"

"Madison," her mom stated firmly. Ana just stared at her, so she said the name again. "Madison Prescott. The love of your life. And speaking of lives, you've got plenty of yours left to live, so maybe you should stop wasting it."

Ana set her fork down and clasped her fingers together. "Mom."

"Don't Mom me, Ana Perez. If you still love her, then do something about it. Take what belongs to you! Get up off that chair and go and get it!"

Ana pushed her chair back and stood up, but she didn't go anywhere; she just stood there, staring at her mom. Then she walked over to the photo of the oak tree and stood in front of it for a moment. "Was she ever really mine?"

"She asked you to marry her. She gave you a ring. And then she had the guts to come and ask for my permission, which I gave. What happened after that was not her fault; it was mine for lying to you about your father. If I had been truthful from the beginning…" Her mom grabbed her napkin and covered her face as she started to cry.

Ana went to her and knelt in front of her. "Mom, you can't blame yourself. George would've found another way to keep us apart."

Her mom dabbed her eyes and took Ana's hand. "And I hate to think what other way he would've found to hurt you. But he's gone now. So, say it out loud, Ana. What do you really want?"

Ana stood up and went back over to the photo. It had been in a small frame for most of its life, sitting on a bedside table next to her bed. It was the one photo she couldn't let go of. She'd burned most of the photos of the two of them together, but the photo of the oak tree stayed with her wherever she'd lived throughout the years.

When Ana had moved into her new apartment, she had the photo framed large enough to earn a spot on a wall in her living room. *Why this photo?* Out of all the photos of her childhood she could have kept, why did she keep a photo of a tree?

But it wasn't just any tree. It was Madison's tree. She turned and looked at her mom. "What if it's too late?"

"It's never too late," her mom said. "Madison deserves real love, not some marriage of convenience. And who in this world do you believe is best equipped to give her that love?"

Ana pointed at herself. "Me," she whispered. "But what if—"

Her mom put up her hand again. "No." She grabbed her purse and pulled out a small piece of scrap paper. "You know I've spent some time in the big house, helping Maddy recover from her wound. I take her lunch sometimes and keep her company. Nothing big, just helping out. And one day, I saw an old CD sitting on her desk. There was a name on it. Your name. I opened it, and there was only one song on the playlist." Her mom held out the piece of paper. "I wrote it down."

Ana took the piece of paper. It said, Alicia Keys – "If I Ain't Got You."

"You have every song known to man on your phone. So, play it," her mom said.

"I don't have this song, but I can buy it." It took Ana less than a minute to buy the song. And then, it was playing on her sound system throughout the apartment. When the song finished, Ana laughed under her breath and wiped away her tears.

Her mom smiled. "So, what are you waiting for? Go get your girl."

❖

Albert sat alone in his favorite diner near the estate. He took the letter out of his pocket and put on his reading glasses. He'd read it one more time and then decide if ruining Madison's holiday weekend was the only possible course of action or if it could wait until Monday.

Dear Albert,

You're probably wondering if I'm really such an asshole that I left you nothing or if I have something else up my sleeve. The latter is true, and you never should've wondered. I'm as loyal to you as you were to me.

I have no doubt that upon your receipt of this letter, my daughter will have already sought out the attentions of a certain woman. I also have no doubt that your affection for her has prevented you from taking the necessary steps to keep the family reputation intact. I don't hold that against you, Albert. You've gone above and beyond the call of duty for me many times. That's why this time, it's not up to you. You've held that burden for long enough. The job will now fall to someone else. I've told him everything he needs to know, and he'll be expecting you soon. Just give him this card, and he'll give you a check. I won't tell you the amount, but you can be sure I've taken good care of you. May I also suggest that you make yourself scarce after you receive this?

Thank you for your valued service.

GP

P.S. He also has a nice box of Cuban cigars for you. Smoke one for me, will you?

George Prescott obviously never expected Albert to transfer his loyalty to Madison once he'd died. That was purely Albert's choice. The letter had arrived the day before with no return address. Albert had no idea what information this attorney, according to the business card, had or what kind of shitstorm George had in mind for his only child. Whatever it was, he figured Ana would suffer the most. Probably lose her job and her good reputation. George had to have known that he couldn't keep them apart in death, so it would just be about making sure their lives were a living hell. George was good at that. Always had been.

Albert didn't like feeling blindsided. He could always take the letter to Madison. Show her once more that her father's love was a twisted, sick, manipulative form of love. She'd take care of Albert. Give him whatever he wanted, most likely. Probably far more than whatever amount was written on that check. George wasn't known for his generosity, after all.

Albert folded the letter and put it in his jacket pocket, leaving the business card sitting on the table. He picked up his cup of coffee and took another sip as he stared at the card. He'd looked the guy up. He was a lowlife who represented shady businessmen. This guy would have no problem implementing George's plan, however sick it might be. He slid the card into his shirt pocket and tossed a five-dollar bill on the table.

The air was crisp and cold. Albert zipped up his jacket and lit a cigarette in the parking lot. He stood by his car while he bounced on his heels and smoked. Something was wrong with this picture; he just couldn't figure out what it was. It didn't make sense that Mr. Prescott would pass this responsibility on to someone else. This was his *only* daughter. His only heir. Why would he trust someone else with her safety? And why not include Albert in the plan? He was the expert on the subject, after all. And why was it a low-life attorney from the Bronx? And the biggest question of all—why did Albert need to make himself scarce?

He'd spent too much time mulling it over. A whole day of wondering what he should do. If he didn't collect the check, would Mr. Prescott have a contingency plan in place for him too, simply because he knew too much? Would something be set in motion where he suddenly disappeared from the face of the earth? No one would miss him. He had no family to speak of, and Mr. Prescott knew that.

What was he missing? He flicked his cigarette across the pavement. It was starting to snow. "What have you done, Mr. Prescott? Whatever it is, she doesn't deserve it. Never did." He stubbed his cigarette out with his foot. "What am I missing?"

And then it hit him. Whatever Mr. Prescott had planned must be too evil for Albert to be trusted with. He'd shown weakness at one point, questioning the plan when he'd seen what it had done to Madison. She was a broken soul for months after they'd made the initial threats. Albert had made the mistake of pointing that out to George. He didn't give a damn. He even said he wished he'd just gotten rid of the problem altogether. Albert gasped at the realization and grabbed for his phone.

Ana's windshield wipers were on full speed trying to deal with the heavy, wet snow coming down. What was she doing? It was crazy to think she'd just waltz onto the estate on Thanksgiving Day and have a heart to heart with Madison. Because really, it wasn't about *getting her girl*. It was about sitting down and having a conversation. Face-to-face. It was about figuring out how to look at each other and see something besides heartbreak and betrayal and pain. They would talk. They would tell each other about their lives. Catch up on the last fifteen years. That was a good place to start.

She pulled over to the side of the road. The guy behind her with his damned brights on was certainly in a hurry. He sped past and turned left onto a side street. Good. She wasn't going to speed down this windy road with the snow coming down like it was.

She was almost there. Just a few more miles to Madison's road.

❖

Scott's mother, Grace, wiped the corners of her mouth with a napkin. "How's everything going with your recovery, dear?" She gave the butler a nod, letting him know he could take her plate.

Madison set her fork down. "Pretty well, actually. I'm getting stronger every day."

"And the company?" Scott's father looked over his glasses at her. "Will it survive the loss of your father?"

"Dad." Scott glared at his father.

Madison put her hand on Scott's knee. "It's okay." She'd always felt as if she'd never truly earned John Fairmont's respect. He was old school, just like George, with one exception: he believed that a woman had no business running a company of that size. He'd never said it out loud, but Madison knew that's what he believed just by some of the things he'd said over the years.

"I suppose the scandal that Nora brought to the family won't help matters," Grace said. "It's all anyone can talk about in my circles."

"And mine," John added. "George would roll over in his grave if he knew."

Madison seethed. Scott's parents had visited her in the hospital exactly once. All they seemed to care about was how the shooting might affect their own standing in the upper echelons of New York society. "George was the cause of the shooting. If he's going to roll over in his grave about something, maybe it should be about that."

Grace pursed her lips and looked to her husband for a reply. He went back to his turkey and stuffing.

❖

Ana's phone rang again. Who the hell was calling her on Thanksgiving Day? She didn't recognize the number, but she hit the button, turning on the speaker phone in her car. "This better not be a sales call."

"Ana, it's Albert. I don't have time for pleasantries."

Ana rolled her eyes. "Since when did you ever care about pleasantries—what the hell!"

"What's wrong? Where are you, Ana?"

"It's nothing. Just a crazy driver." Ana peered through the window. Sure enough, the crappy little sports car that had just sped past her was the same one from before.

"Where are you? I need to know, Ana. It's important."

"You mean, you don't already know? I thought you knew my every damned move. You could probably tell me the exact time and day I go to the hair stylist. When I get a mani-pedi. Where I get my takeout."

"Ana, seriously. We don't have time. Tell me about that crazy driver."

"Shit! Asshole! He just slammed on his brakes and then took off again."

"Ana? Ana! Where are you? What kind of car is it?"

"I'm almost at the estate. What the hell is this guy doing?" Ana watched the driver speed past her again, then flip around so he was behind her. "It's red. A crappy little red car."

"I'm almost there. Stop on the side of the road by the gate, but don't get out of your car. Just wait for me, okay?"

Ana's heart rate sped up. "What's going on?"

"I think you might be in danger. Lock the doors. Stop at the gate. If he stops and approaches you, take off."

"Got it."

❖

Madison desperately wanted the evening to be over, but that wasn't happening. They'd retired to the library where coffee and brandy had been served. The brandy almost guaranteed that John would soon get even more vocal with his politics and misogynistic views on life. *Things to look forward to.*

The curtains were open. She could see the snow coming down hard. It almost felt romantic with the fire burning in the fireplace. Almost.

"John and I think it's time you two considered adoption," Grace said. "It's not the perfect solution by any means, but it's better than nothing."

Madison took a sip of coffee and held the cup in front of her mouth. She wished looks could kill, or at least maim, as she stared Grace down. Scott could handle this one because all that would come out of her mouth was profanities.

"We don't blame you, Madison. We know it's Scott's fault that you don't have children. You could also consider a sperm donor. Possibly someone related. It's up to you, of course."

"Well, thank God you don't blame me. I'd probably throw myself off of a bridge if I thought you considered me barren. I mean, how dare a woman not have children. Am I right?"

Grace started to nod but stopped when she realized Madison was being sarcastic.

❖

Ana froze when she saw the gun. The man had it pointed at her head as he approached her car. She'd pulled over where the Prescott property started, not at the gate where Albert had told her to. Whatever this was, she didn't want to bring it right to Madison's front door.

She hit the gas pedal and swerved around him. A bullet shattered the back window and whizzed past her ear. She screamed and lost control of the car on the wet road. She spun a few times and landed in the ditch that separated the rock wall from the road. She got her bearings and looked around. The gate was just a few feet in front of her. She'd brought it to Madison's door anyway.

The engine was still running, so she hit the gas, but her tires just spun in the muddy snow. She jerked around when she heard a noise. He was behind her, gun pointed at her head again, shouting for her to get out of the car. Where the hell was Albert? He said he was right behind her, but she couldn't see any headlights in either direction.

Another bullet buzzed past her head. She screamed again. "Okay! Don't shoot me! I'll get out of the car!"

"Bring your purse," he shouted.

Her hands were shaking. She grabbed her purse and opened the door. She slipped on the snow and fell to her knees.

"Stay down," he said.

Ana tried to get a good look at the man. He was young. Not more than twenty-five. Baggy jeans and a black down coat. A camo beanie covered his head. He didn't seem to care that she was looking at him while he threw things out of her purse. The cash he slid into his coat pocket.

"Gotta make it look like a robbery," he mumbled.

Oh God. She was as good as dead. She hoped Madison would take care of her mother. Of course she would. It would be okay. She sucked back her emotions and held her head high.

"I got a message for you." The man pointed his gun at her head. "Something I'm supposed to say right before you die." He dug in his back pocket. "Shit. What was it again?"

"George," Ana said, trying to stall him. "It's a message from George, right?"

"Yeah. That's right." He fumbled with his gun and dropped the piece of paper in a puddle of slush on the road. He picked it up and rubbed it against his jeans, smearing the writing. Well, this was just great. *I'm going to be killed by a damned idiot.*

"Damn, it got wet." He put his hands on his hips and looked at the sky. "Now, what the hell was that? Somethin' bout never while he was alive or dead." He shook his head. "I can't remember. Now, look away."

Ana didn't move. "No. If I die, you have to look me in the eyes."

He lunged at her, gun in hand. "I said, turn away, bitch."

The snow was coming down so hard, it was sticking to his eyelashes. Ana laughed at herself for noticing that. For some reason, her fear had subsided. Maybe it was because she knew this day would come. The all-powerful George Prescott would find a way to keep on ruining their lives. Or just end them altogether. "How much did he pay you?"

"Why? You got a better offer?" He motioned with his head at her BMW. "Looks like you got money."

Ana saw movement out of the corner of her eye. "Yeah. I do okay." She resisted the urge to look and see who was coming. "What are we talking? 10K?"

He chuckled and lowered his gun slightly. "You gotta do better than that, pretty lady."

Albert put a gun to the man's head. "Don't move, asshole. I will not hesitate to end your life right here." He took the gun from the man's hand and held him by the collar of his coat.

Ana got up off of her knees. She asked the question again. "How much for my life?"

The man shook his head. "I only know my cut. Five large."

"And you still scoffed when I offered 10K," Ana said.

He grinned. "I knew you'd go higher."

Albert shoved the gun into the guy's back a little harder. "I'll take care of this moron."

Ana stepped up to the guy and dug her money out of his pocket. "You have terrible aim. Two shots into my car and both of them missed me. Makes me think this isn't really your thing, killing people." She balled her fist and hit him in the stomach as hard as she could. "That was for scaring the shit out of me." Then she kneed him in the crotch, causing him to cry out in pain. "And that one's for George Prescott. I figure if you can take his money, you can take a kick in your shriveled-up balls for him too."

Saying the man's name caused the long-held hatred and anger to bubble up to the surface. She lunged at the man, jabbing her finger at him. "You almost killed me for a man who is dead, do you know that?" He didn't reply, so she yelled, "Do you know that, you asshole? The man who hired you hated me simply because I loved his daughter. That's it. That's my big crime." She threw her hands in the air as tears filled her eyes. "And now, it's too late. It's too fucking late for us." She leaned against her car and covered her face with her hands.

Crying wasn't what Ana wanted to be doing right now, but she couldn't stop the tears. No matter what her mom or anyone else thought, this stupid incident was just more proof that she and Madison were doomed from the start and always would be.

They'd both almost died due to his selfishness and hatred. How bad did it have to get before Ana would walk away again? For good this time. She'd never drive down this road again. It was over. Done. She just had to get her car out of the snow first.

"It's not too late."

Ana took her hands from her face and found Albert standing in front of her. He'd handcuffed the guy to the door handle on his car. The asshole grimaced in pain—either from being handcuffed too tightly or from Ana's earlier kickboxing exhibition. Good. Let him hurt a little.

Albert also leaned against Ana's car. "It's not a real marriage. I never reported that information to Mr. Prescott. Didn't feel the need so long as Madison stayed away from you." He shrugged. "But I knew it wasn't love when they married years ago, and from what I've seen, that hasn't changed."

Albert hadn't told Ana anything new. She'd heard the same from Madison. "They're beards. I already know that." She wiped her eyes. "You still making amends, Albert?"

"After the life I've lived? Yeah, I'll never be done. But that's not why I'm telling you the truth about them. I'm doing it because you and Madison belong together and maybe, just maybe, I'd like to see something beautiful for once." He took his cap off and brushed the snow away. "Madison didn't have a choice about any of this. For a long time, I lived in fear that she'd defy George and see you again. If that had happened, it would've been my job to inform *El Serpiente* that he had a daughter he didn't know about. And if you felt like your life had been ruined, well, just imagine what your father would've done to your mother." He turned to her. "God knows I'm no expert on love. Hell, I'm just an ex-cop who used to drink too much." He put his cap back on. "Don't worry about this asshole. He and I will have a good, long talk." He pushed himself off of the car and paused, then reached in his pocket and took out a key fob. He pointed it at the huge security gate, and it slowly opened. "Like I said, I'm no expert on love, but she's in there, waiting for you."

CHAPTER NINETEEN

Ana followed the sound of distant voices to the library.

"I just don't understand why you won't consider John Jr. as a sperm donor."

The voice was deep and unfamiliar. Ana assumed it was Scott's dad.

"It would keep the bloodline in the family."

That voice had to be his mother. She stepped into the room, and all eyes turned to her. "If anyone is going to have a child with Madison, it's going to be me."

It wasn't what she'd intended to say, but having a gun pointed at her head put things into perspective.

Madison and Scott both stood. "Ana," Madison said. "Are you all right?"

Ana glanced at her clothing. Yes, her boots were a little muddy, and her jeans were wet from kneeling in the snow. Madison motioned with her hand to her face. Shit. Ana wiped whatever was on her cheek away and looked at her hand. Great. It was mud. "There was a situation, but I'm fine."

Madison smiled. And that smile turned into a huge grin. "Hi," she said.

"Hi, Maddy. I'm sorry to interrupt, but times a-wastin', ya know?"

The man with the deep voice stood up. He was tall like Scott but not nearly as good looking. "Who is this woman?"

Madison smile hadn't faded. "This is Ana Perez. Ana, this is John and Grace Fairmont." She turned to Scott. "I have to go now."

Scott squeezed her hand. "I know. And I have a story, a long story, for my parents. I'm sure we'll be here a while."

"Take your time, Scott. I'm proud of you." Madison turned to his parents. "Don't forget, he's your son, and he loves you."

Ana held out her hand. Madison took it and followed her to the bottom of the stairs. "I can do stairs now, but we'll have to take it slow."

Ana held her by the hand and wrapped an arm around her. "I got you."

They worked their way up the stairs, and when they got to the top, Madison said, "Where are we going?"

Ana took her hand and led her down the hall. "To the only room I know." She opened the door to Madison's old bedroom. It looked exactly the same with the heavy blue curtains. All of the photos and awards had been removed from the shelves, but everything else felt so familiar to Ana.

She closed the door behind them, and Madison turned to her with a worried look on her face. "What's going on?"

"I'll tell you all about it later, but first, I need to say something. She tucked her hair behind her ears and took a deep breath. "I came here to talk. I thought if we could just talk face-to-face—just get it all out, we could at least be friends. But that's not what I want."

"It's not?"

Ana shook her head. "No."

"Oh." Madison turned away from her and folded her arms. "I'd hoped we could eventually—"

"Maddy, didn't you hear me down there?"

Madison turned back around. "But you just said—"

"I said, I don't want to be friends." She took a step closer. "I want everything. All of it. All the things we used to talk about and dream about. I want the future you promised me when you put that ring on my finger."

Madison seemed unsure, so Ana stepped even closer. "All those questions running through your mind right now, we'll figure it out. We have to."

"I was so naïve when I asked you to marry me. Young and stupid and idealistic. I knew nothing about life, and I had no right to put you in that position. I'm so sorry I did that to us." Madison covered her face and broke down.

"Hey." Ana pulled Madison into her arms. She stroked her hair and let her cry for a moment. "You didn't know what he would do."

"You were right when you said I should've fought for you." Madison wrapped her arms around Ana's waist. "How could I ever have let you go?"

Ana pulled back and cupped Madison's cheeks with both hands. "No, Maddy. You did the right thing. And do you want to know how I know that?" Madison nodded. "Because I just had a gun pointed at my head. A man your father hired just tried to kill me. Luckily, Albert was there to stop him."

"What?" Madison pushed Ana back and looked her up and down. "Are you okay? Is that why you're wet and muddy? My God, Ana. What the hell happened? Where is this man? Where's Albert?"

"He's taking care of it. And he told me to go and get my girl, which is what I'm trying to do. The only question is, am I succeeding?"

Madison ran her hands over Ana's hair and kissed her cheek. "I'm so glad you're okay. Goddamn him."

"Yes. Goddamn him," Ana said. "Personally, I want the ultimate revenge. I want to marry his daughter and live in his home and be a mother to his grandchildren. I want to—"

Madison didn't let her finish. Their lips collided in a slow, tender kiss.

The sounds of sirens emerged from the distance, getting louder as the kiss continued. Ana would need to talk to the officers, of course, but she didn't see any reason the kiss couldn't continue until they arrived.

❖

One month later

Ana had been tickling Madison's backside for going on ten minutes, running her fingers up one side of her body and down the other. "You missed this, didn't you?"

Madison opened her eyes. "You have no idea."

Ana gently bit her shoulder. "And the sex?"

Madison rolled onto her side. "You have no idea."

Christmas was just a few days away. Ana had a tree delivered to her apartment, which they were supposed to decorate together, but they got sidetracked when Ana got up on the ladder to place an ornament near the top. Madison had said the view was too good to pass up. She pulled Ana back down the ladder and ripped her clothes off on the way to the bedroom.

Ana put her finger on Madison's lips and let her take it into her mouth. This was the second time they'd made love since Thanksgiving. Madison was still recovering, so they had to go slow. That was fine with Ana. She wanted time to slow down anyway. She wanted to savor every second they had together. Every moment they looked into each other's eyes felt like a gift. Lying naked in each other's arms felt like a miracle.

Ana pulled her index finger out of Madison's mouth and gave her the middle one. "I love it when you do that."

Madison kissed her finger. "I know. I remember."

Ana pulled her finger away and replaced it with her tongue. She kissed Madison deeply, then took her bottom lip into her mouth. She was so turned on, she wanted her again but knew

Madison probably didn't have the energy for more. She yelped in surprise when Madison rolled them over so she was on top. "What are you doing?" Ana ran her hands down Madison's back and squeezed her ass.

"Do you remember that time in my dorm room when we both came at the same time?"

"Yeah." Ana smiled. "That was the first time we were totally naked together."

"And we were so young we weren't even sure how it had happened."

Ana kissed her way from Madison's lips to her ear. "Friction," she whispered.

Madison giggled. "Yeah." She ground her hips, pushing down on Ana's center. "I'm so turned on, I bet I'd come like that again."

Ana's eyes widened. "I should be on top." She desperately wanted this to happen, but she knew Madison would wear out fast. She rolled them over and sank down in between Madison's legs. If she could make Madison come just by grinding against her, it would make her whole life. Okay, maybe that was an exaggeration, but it would be huge.

Madison wrapped her legs around Ana's body. "I can't get enough of you. Will you move in with me?"

Ana leaned on her elbows and set a slow pace, grinding against Madison's center. "At the estate?"

"We could live at your place if you want. I just want us to be together. Oh God, that feels good."

Ana kept a steady pace. "Can we talk about this later?"

Madison grabbed Ana's face and nodded. "Yeah. Faster."

Ana pushed up off her elbows onto her hands. She quickened the pace. She let her eyes rake over Madison's breasts gently bouncing below her. God, it was a sight to behold. "You're beautiful, Maddy. And I love you so much."

Madison reached up and rubbed her thumb over Ana's bottom lip. "I love you too. Don't stop."

Tears came to Ana's eyes. She hadn't been able to tell anyone that she loved them during sex. And here she was, saying it as if it was no big deal. But it was a big deal. And it wasn't. Because this was Maddy. The girl she was born to love.

Madison ran her hands over Ana's breasts, taking the nipples between her fingers. Ana moaned. She was getting close, but she didn't care if she had an orgasm. She wanted to watch Madison come undone. She wanted to hear it and feel it and remember this moment forever—the moment she was able to say those words again, in the heat of passion.

"Ana." Madison closed her eyes. "Oh God, Ana." She rocked her hips harder. "I'm—oh God!"

Ana slowed her pace to almost nothing until Madison came down from her orgasm. Then, she unlocked her elbows and lay on top of her. She pushed Madison's hair out of the way and whispered in her ear. "You're mine. Forever. No one can take you away again. Not ever."

❖

Ana idled at the stop sign. How many times had she walked Prescott Lane? Rode her bike up and down the curvy road? Jumped off the bus at this very corner? For ten years it was her home. And soon it would be again.

She turned left and raced up the road, suddenly feeling anxious to get there and wrap her arms around the woman she'd loved her whole life. No hesitation. No questioning their past. Just living in the here and now.

The gate opened, and she slowly drove up the road that led to the main house. The ground was covered in snow, and the trees were bare. She found herself looking forward to spring when everything would come alive again. The groundskeeper would be busy, trimming back dead branches and mowing the massive lawn. It would be fun to see what had changed in fifteen years.

Were the lilac bushes by the staff quarters still there? Would the daffodils by the stables pop up in a few months? Only time would tell.

Time. It was time to start living again. She parked in the drive and pulled a weekender bag out of the back seat. When she closed the car door, she saw Madison walking toward her. She grinned. "Hey."

"Hey." Madison kissed Ana's cheek then stood in front of her with her arms folded. "What's the bag for?"

"For tonight. I figure I'll start moving the rest of my things in tomorrow."

"Ana. You don't have to do this. We can live anywhere. It doesn't have to be here. All I care about is having you next to me for the rest of my life."

Ana threw her bag over her shoulder and took Madison's hand. "When the snow melts, I want to go to our tree and take another photo. A selfie that we can frame." They walked to the door at a slow pace even though the air was cold, and they could see their own breath. "Maybe make it something we do every year." She dropped her bag and turned to Madison. "What do you think?"

Madison smiled. "I think it's a great idea. If you're sure."

"I'm sure." Ana took Madison by the arms and pulled her closer. "This is our home. You're my home. Let's be happy here again."

About the Author

Elle Spencer is the author of several best-selling lesbian romances, including the Goldie finalist, *Casting Lacey*. She is a hopeless romantic and firm believer in true love, although she knows the path to happily ever after is rarely an easy one—not for Elle and not for her characters.

Before jumping off a cliff to write full time, Elle ran an online store and worked as a massage therapist. Her wife is especially grateful for the second one. When she's not writing, Elle loves a good home improvement project and reading lots (and lots) of lesfic.

Elle and her wife split their time between Utah and California, ensuring that at any given time they are either too hot or too cold.

Website: http://ellespencerbooks.com

Books Available from Bold Strokes Books

A Bird of Sorrow by Shea Godfrey. As Darrius and her lover, Princess Jessa, gather their strength for the coming war, a mysterious spell will reveal the truth of an ancient love. (978-1-63555-009-2)

All the Worlds Between Us by Morgan Lee Miller. High school senior Quinn Hughes discovers that a broken friendship is actually a door propped open for an unexpected romance. (978-1-63555-457-1)

An Intimate Deception by CJ Birch. Flynn County Sheriff Elle Ashley has spent her adult life atoning for her wild youth, but when she finds her ex, Jessie, murdered two weeks before the small town's biggest social event, she comes face-to-face with her past and all her well-kept secrets. (978-1-63555-417-5)

Cash and the Sorority Girl by Ashley Bartlett. Cash Braddock doesn't want to deal with morality, drugs, or people. Unfortunately, she's going to have to. (978-1-63555-310-9)

Counting for Thunder by Phillip Irwin Cooper. A struggling actor returns to the Deep South to manage a family crisis, finds love, and ultimately his own voice as his mother is regaining hers for possibly the last time. (978-1-63555-450-2)

Falling by Kris Bryant. Falling in love isn't part of the plan, but will Shaylie Beck put her heart first and stick around, or tell the damaging truth? (978-1-63555-373-4)

Secrets in a Small Town by Nicole Stiling. Deputy Chief Mackenzie Blake has one mission: find the person harassing

Savannah Castillo and her daughter before they cause real harm. (978-1-63555-436-6)

Stormy Seas by Ali Vali. The high-octane follow-up to the best-selling action-romance, *Blue Skies*. (978-1-63555-299-7)

The Road to Madison by Elle Spencer. Can two women who fell in love as girls overcome the hurt caused by the father who tore them apart? (978-1-63555-421-2)

Dangerous Curves by Larkin Rose. When love waits at the finish line, dangerous curves are a risk worth taking. (978-1-63555-353-6)

Love to the Rescue by Radclyffe. Can two people who share a past really be strangers? (978-1-62639-973-0)

Love's Portrait by Anna Larner. When museum curator Molly Goode and benefactor Georgina Wright uncover a portrait's secret, public and private truths are exposed, and their deepening love hangs in the balance. (978-1-63555-057-3)

Model Behavior by MJ Williamz. Can one woman's instability shatter a new couple's dreams of happiness? (978-1-63555-379-6)

Pretending in Paradise by M. Ullrich. When travelwisdom.com assigns PR specialist Caroline Beckett and travel blogger Emma Morgan to cover a hot new couples retreat, they're forced to fake a relationship to secure a reservation. (978-1-63555-399-4)

Recipe for Love by Aurora Rey. Hannah Little doesn't have much use for fancy chefs or fancy restaurants, but when New York City chef Drew Davis comes to town, their attraction just might be a recipe for love. (978-1-63555-367-3)

Survivor's Guilt and Other Stories by Greg Herren. Award-winning author Greg Herren's short stories are finally pulled together into a single collection, including the Macavity Award nominated title story and the first-ever Chanse MacLeod short story. (978-1-63555-413-7)

The House by Eden Darry. After a vicious assault, Sadie, Fin, and their family retreat to a house they think is the perfect place to start over, until they realize not all is as it seems. (978-1-63555-395-6)

Uninvited by Jane C. Esther. When Aerin McLeary's body becomes host for an alien intent on invading Earth, she must work with researcher Olivia Ando to uncover the truth and save humankind. (978-1-63555-282-9)

Comrade Cowgirl by Yolanda Wallace. When cattle rancher Laramie Bowman accepts a lucrative job offer far from home, will her heart end up getting lost in translation? (978-1-63555-375-8)

Double Vision by Ellie Hart. When her cell phone rings, Giselle Cutler answers it—and finds herself speaking to a dead woman. (978-1-63555-385-7)

Inheritors of Chaos by Barbara Ann Wright. As factions splinter and reunite, will anyone survive the final showdown between gods and mortals on an alien world? (978-1-63555-294-2)

Love on Lavender Lane by Karis Walsh. Accompanied by the buzz of honeybees and the scent of lavender, Paige and Kassidy must find a way to compromise on their approach to business if they want to save Lavender Lane Farm—and find a way to make room for love along the way. (978-1-63555-286-7)

Spinning Tales by Brey Willows. When the fairy tale begins to unravel and villains are on the loose, will Maggie and Kody be able to spin a new tale? (978-1-63555-314-7)

The Do-Over by Georgia Beers. Bella Hunt has made a good life for herself and put the past behind her. But when the bane of her high school existence shows up for Bella's class on conflict resolution, the last thing they expect is to fall in love. (978-1-63555-393-2)

What Happens When by Samantha Boyette. For Molly Kennan, senior year is already an epic disaster, and falling for mysterious waitress Zia is about to make life a whole lot worse. (978-1-63555-408-3)

Wooing the Farmer by Jenny Frame. When fiercely independent modern socialite Penelope Huntingdon-Stewart and traditional country farmer Sam McQuade meet, trusting their hearts is harder than it looks. (978-1-63555-381-9)

A Chapter on Love by Laney Webber. When Jannika and Lee reunite, their instant connection feels like a gift, but neither is ready for a second chance at love. Will they finally get on the same page when it comes to love? (978-1-63555-366-6)

Drawing Down the Mist by Sheri Lewis Wohl. Everyone thinks Grand Duchess Maria Romanova died in 1918. They were almost right. (978-1-63555-341-3)

Listen by Kris Bryant. Lily Croft is inexplicably drawn to Hope D'Marco but will she have the courage to confront the consequences of her past and present colliding? (978-1-63555-318-5)

Perfect Partners by Maggie Cummings. Elite police dog trainer Sara Wright has no intention of falling in love with a coworker, until Isabel Marquez arrives at Homeland Security's Northeast Regional Training facility and Sara's good intentions start to falter. (978-1-63555-363-5)

Shut Up and Kiss Me by Julie Cannon. What better way to spend two weeks of hell in paradise than in the company of a hot, sexy woman? (978-1-63555-343-7)

Spencer's Cove by Missouri Vaun. When Foster Owen and Abigail Spencer meet they uncover a story of lives adrift, loves lost, and true love found. (978-1-63555-171-6)

Without Pretense by TJ Thomas. After living for decades hiding from the truth, can Ava learn to trust Bianca with her secrets and her heart? (978-1-63555-173-0)

Unexpected Lightning by Cass Sellars. Lightning strikes once more when Sydney and Parker fight a dangerous stranger who threatens the peace they both desperately want. (978-1-163555-276-8)

Emily's Art and Soul by Joy Argento. When Emily meets Andi Marino she thinks she's found a new best friend but Emily doesn't know that Andi is fast falling in love with her. Caught up in exploring her sexuality, will Emily see the only woman she needs is right in front of her? (978-1-63555-355-0)

Escape to Pleasure: Lesbian Travel Erotica edited by Sandy Lowe and Victoria Villasenor. Join these award-winning authors as they explore the sensual side of erotic lesbian travel. (978-1-63555-339-0)

Music City Dreamers by Robyn Nyx. Music can bring lovers together. In Music City, it can tear them apart. (978-1-63555-207-2)

Ordinary is Perfect by D. Jackson Leigh. Atlanta marketing superstar Autumn Swan's life derails when she inherits a country home, a child, and a very interesting neighbor. (978-1-63555-280-5)

Royal Court by Jenny Frame. When royal dresser Holly Weaver's passionate personality begins to melt Royal Marine Captain Quincy's icy heart, will Holly be ready for what she exposes beneath? (978-1-63555-290-4)

Strings Attached by Holly Stratimore. Success. Riches. Music. Passion. It's a life most can only dream of, but stardom comes at a cost. (978-1-63555-347-5)

The Ashford Place by Jean Copeland. When Isabelle Ashford inherits an old house in small-town Connecticut, family secrets, a shocking discovery, and an unexpected romance complicate her plan for a fast profit and a temporary stay. (978-1-63555-316-1)

Treason by Gun Brooke. Zoem Malderyn's existence is a deadly threat to everyone on Gemocon and Commander Neenja KahSandra must find a way to save the woman she loves from having to commit the ultimate sacrifice. (978-1-63555-244-7)

BOLDSTROKESBOOKS.COM

Looking for your next great read?

Visit BOLDSTROKESBOOKS.COM
to browse our entire catalog of paperbacks, ebooks,
and audiobooks.

Want the first word on what's new?
Visit our website for event info,
author interviews, and blogs.

Subscribe to our free newsletter for sneak peeks,
new releases, plus first notice of promos
and daily bargains.

SIGN UP AT
BOLDSTROKESBOOKS.COM/signup

Bold Strokes Books

Quality and Diversity in LGBTQ Literature

*Bold Strokes Books is an award-winning publisher
committed to quality and diversity in LGBTQ fiction.*